Hooky

VOLUME 3

MÍRIAM BONASTRE TUR

CLARION BOOKS

IMPRINTS OF HARPERCOLLINSPUBLISHERS

CLARION BOOKS IS AN IMPRINT OF HARPERCOLLINS PUBLISHERS.
HARPERALLEY IS AN IMPRINT OF HARPERCOLLINS PUBLISHERS.

HOOKY VOLUME 3
COPYRIGHT © 2023 BY MÍRIAM BONASTRE TUR

ISBN 978-0-35-869358-1 — ISBN 978-0-35-869357-4 (PBK.)
ISBN 978-0-06-334183-8 (SIGNED EDITION)

LETTERING BY NATALIE FONDRIEST

PB: 23-WOZ-3
HC: 23-WOZ-2

FIRST EDITION
A DIGITAL VERSION OF *HOOKY* WAS ORIGINALLY PUBLISHED ON
WEBTOON IN 2015.

4

9

11

IT MEANS THAT I'LL DO EVERYTHING I CAN TO MAKE YOU FEEL MORE LIKE YOUR OLD SELF.

GET OUT OF MY SIGHT.

BUT DANI, WHAT...?

DON'T CALL ME DANI. I'M YOUR QUEEN.

EVEN IF IT PAINS YOU TO ADMIT THAT, BECAUSE I KNOW YOU ONLY WISH TO SEE ALL WITCHES FALL,

TO SEE OUR KIND MARGINALIZED AND MURDERED. I WON'T ALLOW IT.

...SEE YOU SOON.

LISTEN, GIRL...

DON'T GET RID OF HIM YET.

WHY?

HE COULD BE USEFUL TO US IN THE FUTURE.

MOREOVER, YOUR DESPAIR IS DELICIOUS.

I THOUGHT YOU DIDN'T WANT TO MARRY ME!

CALM DOWN, MONICA.

YOU HAVE TO DO THIS.

HE'S NOT COMING BACK ANYWAY.

THUMP THUMP

HE LEFT.

HE SAID HE'D BE BACK SOON.

THAT WAS THE LAST TIME I SAW DORIAN.

SINCE THEN, THINGS HAVE GOTTEN WORSE.

THERE WAS A BIG FIGHT BETWEEN THE SORCERERS AND KING EDGAR'S SOLDIERS.

MANY DIED, BUT DANI AND HER MOTHER FLED BEFORE I COULD SEE HER AND TELL HER WHAT HAD REALLY HAPPENED.

19

NICO SNEAKED OUT AS OFTEN AS HE COULD

GIVING US UPDATES ABOUT DANI AND ASKING FOR HELP.

BUT WE COULDN'T GET CLOSE TO HER.

EVERY TIME THE KING SENT A MESSENGER OR A SPY, THEY ENDED UP BURNED AT THE GATES OF THE CITY.

AT A CERTAIN POINT, I DECIDED TO ACT.

I WANTED TO DO SOMETHING TO SAVE DANI.

I RESEARCHED, PRACTICED, AND BECAME STRONGER.

MARRYING WILLIAM IS ESSENTIAL TO SECURE THE SUPPORT OF THE NOBILITY AND THE PEOPLE

AND TO OBTAIN THE FULL STRENGTH OF THE ARMIES OF BOTH KINGDOMS.

THE PROMISE OF LOVE I MADE TO DORIAN

HAS FALLEN SO FAR BEHIND ME IN TIME THAT IT NOW SEEMS LIKE CHILD'S PLAY.

IT HAS BEEN THREE YEARS SINCE HE LEFT

AND MY MEMORIES OF THAT TIME HAVE SLOWLY FADED.

AFTER ALL, I ONLY SPENT ONE YEAR OF MY LIFE WITH DORIAN.

I DON'T EVEN KNOW ANYMORE WHAT PART OF HIM IS REAL...

...AND WHAT PART IS JUST AN IDEALIZED MEMORY.

EVEN THOUGH...

SOMETIMES I STILL DREAM ABOUT HIM

ABOUT TALKING AND LAUGHING TOGETHER

AND WHEN I WAKE UP, I FEEL VERY LONELY.

MONICA?

I THOUGHT YOU DIDN'T WANT TO MARRY ME!

YOU SAID NO EVERY SINGLE TIME MY FATHER MENTIONED IT!

IF I HAD MARRIED YOU, YOUR FATHER WOULD'VE USED THAT AS AN EXCUSE TO CLAIM MY FATHER'S KINGDOM!

HE WOULD'VE ENTERED IT WITH HIS ARMY TO KILL ALL THE WITCHES!

HE WOULD'VE HARMED DANI AS WELL AS OTHER INNOCENTS.

I WILL DEFEAT THE QUEEN, DANI, BUT I WANNA DO IT MY OWN WAY.

DO YOU THINK YOU CAN HEAL HER?

I HOPE SO.

THIS HAS BEEN THE MAIN FOCUS OF MY STUDIES. AN ANTIDOTE FOR DANI.

I KNOW.

PERFECT, THEN! I'LL TELL YOU MY PLAN IN MORE DETAIL, WILL, BUT FIRST...

WE HAVE A WEDDING TO PLAN! WE'RE GETTING MARRIED IN TWO WEEKS!

LOOKS LIKE I'M FINALLY GETTING MARRIED, DAMIEN!

CONGRATULATIONS...?

EVEN THOUGH I DON'T THINK I'LL BE ABLE TO ATTEND YOUR WEDDING.

WHAAAAT?! WHY IS THAT?! YOU MUST BE THERE!

THE THING IS... TOMORROW I'LL LEAVE AGAIN WITH MARK AND AISHA.

IT LOOKS LIKE WE MIGHT BE ABLE TO FIND DORIAN THIS TIME.

WHAT? WHY DO YOU THINK THIS TIME WILL BE DIFFERENT?

AISHA TOLD ME THAT THEY RECEIVED A VISIT FROM SOMEONE WE CAN TRUST.

AND THEY BROUGHT A SIGNIFICANT CLUE.

ALL RIGHT, THIS WAY...

WE'VE GOT RICE AND LENTILS, BUT ALSO SOME POTATOES AND CARROTS LEFT.

DID YOU MANAGE TO FIND MILK, MARK?

NOT YET, MR. LOPEZ.

SOME THINGS ARE JUST IMPOSSIBLE TO FIND.

TRADERS DON'T COME HERE THAT OFTEN ANYMORE.

DESPITE THAT, WE BROUGHT A LOT OF FRUIT.

AWESOME!

CAREFUL, LIKE SO...

OH NO, IT BROKE!

YOU NEED TO BE VERY GENTLE WHEN YOU REMOVE THE MOLD!

IF YOU'RE NOT PATIENT, YOU'LL NEVER BE ABLE TO MAKE ONE OF OUR FAMOUS EVANS-CAFÉ-STYLE APPLE PIES!

BUT IT CAN STILL BE EATEN, RIGHT?!

I DON'T THINK PEOPLE WILL MIND IF IT'S A BIT CRUMBLED...!

AH!

PENDRAGON, MY OLD FRIEND!

HELLO, EVANS.

I'M SORRY I VANISHED LIKE THAT... I KNOW YOU ALL NEEDED ME...

THE ONLY THING THAT MATTERS IS THAT YOU'RE OK. WE THOUGHT YOU WERE DEAD!

I DIDN'T COME BACK FOR PLEASURE, THERE'S STILL SOMETHING I NEED TO DO...

I CAN'T HIDE THIS ANYMORE...

CARLO'S JOURNEY

3 YEARS AGO

HOW CHILLY...

MARK, WE SHOULD GO BACK.

WE'VE BEEN OUTSIDE FOR TOO LONG, THERE'S NO TRACE OF DORIAN...

NO! WE CAN'T JUST LEAVE HIM!

WHY ISN'T HE HERE?!

WHAT IF SOMETHING HAPPENED TO HIM?! WHAT IF HE NEEDS OUR HELP...?!

DO YOU THINK HE'S...? UH...

BUT THIS IS SO FRUSTRATING!

WE'LL FIND HIM!

BUT FIRST, WE NEED TO GO BACK. WE'RE ALMOST OUT OF FOOD AND WE DON'T HAVE ANY LEADS.

EH, MARK, LISTEN, I DON'T...!

I'M SORRY, I DIDN'T MEAN THAT!

I KNOW.

WHO KNOWS, PERHAPS HE HAS ALREADY RESCUED DANI AND THEY'RE BOTH SAFE, AT HOME.

DO YOU THINK SO...?

I DON'T KNOW.

BUT WE NEED TO LEAVE.

...ALL RIGHT THEN.

COME ON, CARLO, LET'S GET GOING!

WE SHOULD PROBABLY GO TO THE CAFÉ...

OH! WILL I MEET YOUR FATHER THEN?

DOES HE LOOK LIKE YOU, MARK?

HE'S MORE MUSCULAR, BUT YE....

AAAARGH!!

LET GO, CARLO!

WHAT IS GOING ON WITH YOU?!

LET GOOO!

...

HEY CARLO, BEHAVE! YOU MUST UNDERSTAND THAT WE CAN'T FIND DORIAN IN THESE CONDITIONS!

SO DON'T BE SILLY AND BEHAVE! ALL RIGHT?

DON'T TALK TO HIM LIKE THAT!

ALL RIGHT YOU SILLY FROG, GO AWAY!

WE DON'T NEED YOU!

CARLO, COME BACK!

CARLO!

31

WELL, DAMIEN.

IT LOOKS LIKE I'LL BE A MARRIED MAN NEXT TIME WE MEET.

YEAH, RIGHT...

I'M SORRY I CAN'T COME TO YOUR WEDDING.

DAMIEN,

I NEED YOU TO DO ME A FAVOR.

WHAT IS IT?

I'VE BEEN THINKING ABOUT IT...

IT WOULDN'T BE THE FIRST TIME WE THINK WE'VE FOUND A CLUE AND IT ENDS IN NOTHING.

PEOPLE ARE SUFFERING AND I DON'T WANT TO POSTPONE IT.

SO I'LL GO AHEAD WITH MY PLAN.

YES, YOU MUST STICK TO THE PLAN.

THE TRUTH IS THAT I DON'T HAVE MUCH HOPE EITHER, BUT WE HAVE TO TRY.

HOWEVER...

IF YOU FIND HIM, PLEASE TELL HIM TO COME BACK.

I'M REALLY EAGER TO SEE DORIAN AGAIN.

 LET'S GO, CARLO.

READY?

THAT GUY, JUST NOW... WAS THAT MAGIC?

 GOOD LUCK, GUYS.

BE CAREFUL.

YES, DAD.

WE'LL STILL BE HERE, RESISTING!

I'M COMING WITH YOU.

MASTER!

 I THINK THAT'S PRETTY COOL!

AH, I THINK I CAN HELP WITH THAT.

EH?

I'LL DEFEAT THAT DRAGON!

IT'S NOT THE FIRST TIME I FACED ONE!

I'M COMING WITH YOU! WE'LL BEAT IT UP!

NO, WAIT.

AISHA.

NOT A CHANCE!

HOLD IT THERE!

POW

ARGH!

UGH...

YOU'RE REALLY DUMB, MARK.

NOBODY NEEDS TO DIRECTLY FACE THE DRAGON.

WE'LL USE THE DUMMY AS A BAIT. AS SOON AS IT GETS DISTRACTED, WE'LL GIVE DORIAN THE ANTIDOTE!

ALL RIGHT, DAMIEN...

IN ORDER TO GET THE ANTIDOTE, WE MUST FIGURE OUT THE TYPE OF VENOM...

ISN'T THAT RIGHT, PENDRAGON?

... HE'S DEAD, GUYS.

I'M SORRY, BUT YOU MUST ACCEPT THAT.

DID YOU FIND ANYTHING, DAMIEN?

I'M LOOKING THROUGH MONICA'S STUDIES ON POTIONS.

THEY ARE VERY THOROUGH,

BUT I CAN'T FIND ANY ANTIDOTE TO THE POISON MASTER PENDRAGON GAVE DORIAN.

SO, I CHOSE A GENERAL HEALING POTION.

BUT, MONICA HIGHLIGHTED THIS PARTICULAR RECIPE.

SHE EVEN ADDED A LOT OF EXCLAMATION MARKS AND LITTLE STARS.

IT'S USED TO HEAL MINOR SPELLS, DIFFERENT TYPES OF WOUNDS...

HOW'S IT GOING?

DON'T MAKE HIM NERVOUS, IT'S A DELICATE MOMENT.

WHOA!

AH, OF COURSE!

I KNOW THAT POTION!

I REMEMBER WHEN THEY MADE IT FOR THE FIRST TIME!

48

49

THIS WAY HE CAN JOIN US.

OH, HOW CUTE! YOU SHOULD GIVE THE LITTLE DRAGON A NAME!

YOU WANTED TO KILL IT A FEW MINUTES AGO, AISHA.

LOOK, CARLO'S ABOUT TO CRUSH HIM NOW!

HEY GUYS, CALM DOWN!

HA HA HA HA HA HA HA HA HA HA HA

DORIAN!

HURRY UP, HELP ME LIFT HIM!

OH...

MAGIC? THAT'S HOW CURSES WORK.

PRINCE WILLIAM WAS ALSO IN A DEEP SLUMBER FOR MONTHS AND HE DIDN'T STARVE TO DEATH.

RIGHT, BUT DORIAN GREW UP...

LOOK AT HIM, HE'S TALLER, HE GOT BIGGER. HE MUST HAVE EATEN SOMETHING.

DO YOU WANT ME TO CARRY DORIAN FOR A BIT, MARK?

NO, DON'T WORRY, HE WEIGHS PRACTICALLY NOTHING.

YES, HE'S SO THIN... YOU CAN CLEARLY SEE HE HASN'T EATEN IN YEARS.

HOW CAN HE POSSIBLY BE ALIVE, THEN?

I BET THE DRAGON WAS TAKING CARE OF HIM. GIVING HIM REGURGITATED FOOD!

JUST LIKE MOTHER BIRDS WHEN THEY FEED THEIR BABIES!

AISHA...

YUCK...

NO...

IT WAS MAGIC, WASN'T IT?

I KNOW! AND IT'S ALL BECAUSE OF THIS STUPID WAR BETWEEN WITCHES AND ANTI-WITCHCRAFT PEOPLE!

WITHOUT THEIR NONSENSE, WE WOULD BE SUCH A PROSPEROUS COUNTRY!

AND THESE FIELDS WOULD BE FULL OF SCHOOLS, HOSPITALS, LIBRARIES AND MANY, MANY PUBS!

IF ONLY THEY'D LET ME LEARN MAGIC, I'D PUT EVERYONE RIGHT BACK INTO LINE!

YOU! STOP CHATTERING AND GET BACK TO WORK!

THE BRIDGE WON'T BUILD ITSELF!!

SLAP

AND YOU, GUYS, IF YOU'RE LOOKING FOR A PLACE TO STAY, JUST GO SOUTH.

YOU'LL BE AT THE VILLAGE IN THREE HOURS.

THANKS A LOT, SIR!

GOOD LUCK!

EH... DID YOU NOTICE?

THOSE DUDES... THOSE DUDES WEREN'T WITCHES, OF COURSE. BUT THEY DIDN'T SEEM AFRAID OF MAGIC.

AH, THAT'S TRUE!

YES, I'VE ALSO NOTICED THAT! HOW COOL!

YEAH, IT'S...

IT'S WEIRD.

BESIDES, THIS VILLAGE WAS PROBABLY TAKEN BY DANI'S ARMY... MANY PEOPLE LIVE ON THE STREET,

HALF OF THE BUILDINGS WERE BURNT DOWN.

THEY'VE BEEN THROUGH QUITE A LOT, AND THEY SEEM AFRAID OF THE QUEEN AND HER PEOPLE, YET...

...

EH, THEY SAID THERE ARE VACANT ROOMS!

TELLING DORIAN WHAT HAPPENED.

MAKING HIM UNDERSTAND THAT HE'S BEEN ASLEEP FOR THREE YEARS.

AWESOME! WE'RE LUCKY!

TOMORROW WE'LL HAVE TO DEAL WITH A COMPLICATED MISSION.

AND WHAT IS THAT...?

DO YOU THINK HE'LL TAKE IT WELL? OR WILL HE GO CRAZY?

YES, HE'LL MANAGE.

I'M SURE HE'LL HELP US ALL WITH DANI.

SO... ARE YOU HUNGRY?

DO YOU WANNA GO DOWN AND EAT SOMETHING?

YEAH, I'M STARVING.

WHAT ARE WE GONNA DO WITH THIS ONE, THEN?

YEAH... WE CAN'T GO DOWN WITH THE MASTER TIED UP LIKE A CRIMINAL...

WE'RE WALKING AROUND WITH AN OLD MAN TIED UP AND SOME KIND OF PASSED-OUT ZOMBIE ON OUR BACKS. I'M ACTUALLY SURPRISED THEY DIDN'T CALL THE GUARDS!

BUT WE CAN'T RISK UNTYING HIM. WE NEED TO KEEP AN EYE ON HIM FOR NOW.

TOMORROW MORNING WE'LL HEAD TO MONICA'S CASTLE, AND WE'LL LOCK HIM UP IN THE DUNGEON.

HEY, DON'T TALK AS IF I'M NOT EVEN HERE...

SINCE WE WILL BE TAKING PENDRAGON TO THE DUNGEON, IT LOOKS LIKE WE WILL ACTUALLY BE ABLE TO ATTEND WILLIAM AND MONICA'S WEDDING.

OH, THAT'S COOL!

MY BROTHER AND MOTHER WILL DEFINITELY BE THERE!

HERE'S WHAT YOU'VE ASKED FOR.

THANKS!

OH, AND JUST A QUESTION...

ARE YOU WITCHES, BY ANY CHANCE?

59

DORIAN DISAPPEARED!! HE'S NOT HERE!!

ARE YOU KIDDING ME?!

OH, HE WAS KIDNAPPED!

WHERE IS THAT IDIOT?!

MMH?

OH...?

AH, GUYS, YOU FINALLY WOKE UP!

61

62

PERFECT, I LOOK SO MUCH BETTER!

NOW I CAN RECOGNIZE MYSELF!

EVEN THOUGH SOMETHING IS STILL OFF...

EH... EXCUSE ME... HOW OLD DO I LOOK?

WELL, I DON'T KNOW... SIXTEEN? SEVENTEEN?

SIXTEEN?!

THAT MEANS I SLEPT FOR THREE YEARS??

IS SHE ALIVE...?

AGH... I NEED TO KNOW...

BUT I CAN'T JUST ASK... I DON'T KNOW ABOUT THE CURRENT SITUATION.

I DON'T EVEN KNOW WHAT YEAR IT IS OR WHERE I AM. IT COULD BE DANGEROUS.

I'LL JUST GO WAKE UP NICO AND THE OTHERS... OR...

I HAVE AN IDEA.

DO YOU HAVE A NEWSPAPER BY ANY CHANCE?

WHAT?

A NEWSPAPER?

...

... NO.

THERE'S NO SUCH THING HERE, I DON'T KNOW WHERE YOU GOT THAT INFORMATION.

PLEASE LEAVE.

WHA...?

IT'S FIVE FOR THE HAIRCUT.

AH... I DON'T HAVE ANY MONEY ON ME...

WHAT?!

DID YOU THINK WE'D WORK FOR FREE BECAUSE OF YOUR PRETTY FACE?!

PAY US!!

UHM...

I CAN FIX YOUR WINDOW, IF YOU WANT.

BUT YOU'LL NEED TO LEAVE ME ALONE FOR A SECOND.

I PROMISE I WON'T RUN AWAY.

BUT PLEASE, DON'T COME BACK UNTIL I TELL YOU TO DO SO.

I LOCKED THE DOOR. LET HIM TRY ANYTHING HE WANTS.

... SERIOUSLY, THIS GUY...?

OOOOH...

INCREDIBLE...

WELL, I HOPE THIS WORKS AS A PAYMENT!

THANK YOU SO MUCH FOR EVERYTHING!

HE'S A WITCH.

DOES HE THINK WE'RE STUPID??

...

WHO WAS IT?! WHO WAS HIDING IN THE SWAMP?!

TELL US ALREADY, DORIAN!

YOU DON'T NEED TO RECOUNT YOUR MORNING IN FULL DETAIL!

EH? IT'S QUITE IMPORTANT.

IN THE END, IT TURNED OUT EVERYONE WAS TRYING TO HELP ME, EVEN IF I COULDN'T SEE THAT.

LOOK, I FOUND THE NEWSPAPER.

HMMM...? THIS NEWSPAPER IS...?

ARE THERE ANY ARTICLES ABOUT WITCHCRAFT?

"WEEKLY RECIPE: THIS POTION WILL MAKE YOUR POTATOES GROW IN JUST A FEW HOURS."

WHAT IS THIS...?

THE INSURGENT WITCH

AH! TAKE A LOOK AT THE COVER, MARK...!!

HE INSURGENT WITCH

WHAT'S THIS DRAWING RIGHT HERE...?

IT'S ALEX!!

WHAT'S THIS ALL ABOUT?!

... OH!

HEY!

HI MARK! NICO! LONG TIME NO SEE.

YOU BOTH GREW UP SO FAST!

NOAH! BARRY! WHAT ARE YOU DOING HERE?!

DO YOU LIKE OUR SECRET NEWSPAPER?

GENT WITCH

BUT... WHAT IS IT?

IT'S AN ILLEGAL PUBLICATION.

WE THINK THAT THE WITCH'S REIGN IS ONLY ADDING MORE TROUBLE TO THE CONFLICT.

AND WE WANTED TO OFFER A DIFFERENT PERSPECTIVE,

TO SHOW THAT WITCHES DON'T AGREE WITH THE WYTTES' POLICIES.

WELL... MOST OF THE WYTTES.

SORRY, DORIAN.

IT'S OK.

WE PUBLISHED IT FOR THE PEOPLE. ALL OF THE PEOPLE.

WE'RE TRYING TO KEEP IT A SECRET SINCE WE'D END UP AT THE STAKE IF DANI'S ARMY CATCHES US.

I KNOW I WAS ASLEEP FOR THREE YEARS, FOR SOME REASON.

AND I KNOW THAT DURING THIS TIME, DANI HAS BECOME EVIL.

THEY SAID SHE'S A COLD, CRUEL QUEEN AND THAT SHE DID HORRIBLE THINGS, SHE KILLED PEOPLE.

BUT I DON'T BELIEVE IT.

IT ALL HAS TO DO WITH MY MOTHER.

AND I WILL GO RESCUE HER TODAY.

DORIAN...!

YOU'RE RIGHT, DORIAN. DANI ISN'T EVIL.

BUT SHE IS COLD.

IT'S ALMOST AS IF...

AS IF SHE WERE NOT HERSELF ANYMORE...

SHE HAS BEEN ABSENT SINCE THE MOMENT SHE THOUGHT YOU WERE DEAD.

SO IT'S MY FAULT...

I FAILED HER.

73

THREE YEARS... I CAN'T BELIEVE IT.

I PROMISED I WOULD GET HER OUT OF THERE AND IT TOOK ME THREE YEARS...

IT'S NOT YOUR FAULT, DORIAN!

NO! IT'S...

IT'S THE MASTER'S FAULT.

BUT NOW THAT YOU'RE HERE, EVERYTHING WILL BE FINE!

I KNOW YOU'RE THE ONLY ONE WHO CAN MAKE DANI COME BACK TO HER SENSES!

SHE'LL GO BACK TO NORMAL AS SOON AS SHE SEES YOU!

YES... I THINK SO TOO.

ALL IS NOT LOST, IT SEEMS...

NOT EVERYONE HATES WITCHES...

ACTUALLY, IT'S PRETTY WEIRD BUT PEOPLE SEEM TO BE A LOT LESS FRIGHTENED NOW!

THAT'S BECAUSE PEOPLE ONLY WANT TO LIVE IN PEACE.

THAT'S SOMETHING WE HAVE IN COMMON.

UM... YES...

TRUTH IS, I'VE GIVEN THIS MATTER A LOT OF THOUGHT...

AND I'VE GOT A SERIOUS PROBLEM....

WHAT PROBLEM?

HOW OLD IS MONICA NOW?

EIGHTEEN, JUST LIKE ME.

SHE'S AN ADULT!

HOW AM I SUPPOSED TO TALK TO HER NOW?!

DON'T WORRY, SHE'S DYING TO SEE YOU.

PRECISELY! I'VE MADE HER WAIT THREE YEARS. IT'S ONLY BEEN A WHILE FOR ME.

I BET SHE'S FURIOUS!

OH, MONICA, THOSE EARRINGS WILL LOOK WONDERFUL WITH YOUR WEDDING DRESS!

COME ON, ANNE! THEY LOOK TERRIBLE!

THESE ONES SUIT HER BETTER. THEY'RE MORE DELICATE AND ELEGANT.

LET MONICA DECIDE!

COME ON! WHICH ONE'S THE BEST?

THE ONES I CHOSE FOR YOU, RIGHT?

....

MONICA, ANSWER!

I'M SORRY, GIRLS. I HAVE TO GO!!

HUH? WHERE ARE YOU GOING?!

YOU CAN'T GO OUT LIKE THIS! YOU'RE NAKED!

MMMH??

AH! DAMIEN?!

DAMIEN!!

ARE YOU ALREADY BACK?!

HI, MONICA.

AH...

THAT SMILE...

HOW DID IT GO?

WHERE ARE THE OTHERS?

MONICA... LISTEN.

WE FOUND DORIAN.

HE'S ALIVE AND WELL.

VERY STRONG AND DETERMINED TO SAVE DANI.

DORIAN...!

UH...

HERE, I'LL HELP YOU WITH THAT. YOU SEEM QUITE LONELY.

AND YOU SEEM VERY HAPPY.

... OF COURSE.

WE FOUND DORIAN, SAFE AND SOUND.

AT THIS VERY MOMENT HE'S GOING TO RESCUE DANI. LOOKS PROMISING.

...IS THE WEDDING STILL THAT URGENT, THEN? YES.

IF DORIAN DOESN'T SUCCEED, WE'VE GOT MONICA'S PLAN.

WE CAN'T SUDDENLY CALL OFF THE WEDDING, SPOILING THE WHOLE PLAN.

MOREOVER, SOONER OR LATER, YOU WOULD'VE ENDED UP MARRYING MONICA ANYWAYS, YOU'VE ALWAYS KNOWN THAT.

DOES IT BOTHER YOU? MY WEDDING, I MEAN.

WHY WOULD IT BOTHER ME?

YOU SAID IT YOURSELF, NOTHING WILL CHANGE. WE'LL STILL BE FRIENDS AS USUAL.

BUT DAMIEN,

WHAT IS IT THAT YOU WANT?

WHAT DO YOU WANT, WILL?

THAT DOESN'T ANSWER MY QUESTION.

BONG BONG

BONG BONG

BONG

WHAT DO I WANT...?

I NEED TO MARRY PRINCESS MONICA.

IT'S IMPORTANT TO THE KINGDOM.

YET YOU'VE CHOSEN TO RESCUE DANI INSTEAD OF TRYING TO STOP THE WEDDING.

IT MAKES SENSE.

WHAT HAPPENED BETWEEN US TOOK PLACE A LONG TIME AGO...

IT WAS JUST CHILD'S PLAY...

AND NOW...

I'M ABOUT TO BECOME A MARRIED WOMAN.

I HAVE EVERYTHING PLANNED DOWN TO THE LAST DETAIL.

THE PERFECT DRESS.

THE IDEAL BANQUET.

THE PEOPLE ARE EUPHORIC.

91

KILL HER NOW, DANI!

HURRY UP AND KILL QUEEN MONICA!

UGH...

NO...

PLEASE, REMEMBER...

IT'S ME, MONICA!

THIS CAN'T BE...

IS SHE REALLY LIKE THIS BECAUSE SHE THOUGHT DORIAN HAD DIED?

DIE.

UH... THAT DIDN'T WORK...

WELL, I'VE GOT A BETTER IDEA...

102

AH... SHE GOT AWAY.

SHE DESTROYED THE CATHEDRAL... MONICA'S PLAN DIDN'T WORK, IN THE END...

...

WE'LL NEED TO MOVE ON TO PLAN B AND USE OUR JOINED ARMIES.

WE'LL HAVE WAY MORE SUPPORT NOW THAT WE'RE MARRIED.

THAT'S NOT TRUE...

MY PLAN ACTUALLY DID SOMETHING.

ISN'T THAT TRUE, MRS. WYTTE...?

WE'RE ALMOST THERE! I CAN'T BELIEVE IT; I'LL FINALLY SEE DANI!

WOW... I REMEMBERED THIS PALACE WAY... BRIGHTER.

HAVE YOU BEEN HERE BEFORE?

OF COURSE! I'VE SPENT MANY SUMMERS HERE.

MY BROTHER AND I WOULD SPEND THE DAY PLAYING WITH MONICA, WILL, DAMIEN, IVY AND ANNE.

OH, I WAS ONLY HERE ONCE.

THE DAY OF THE GREAT BALL THE KING ORGANIZED IN HOPES OF REESTABLISHING PEACE DURING THE WAR AGAINST WITCHES...

IT DIDN'T GO WELL.

CLEARLY.

WHAT MATTERS THE MOST IS HOW MARK WAS DRESSED THAT DAY!

I'LL REMEMBER THOSE SILLY LITTLE PINK PANTS 'TIL THE DAY I DIE!

HA-HA!

BUT...

WHERE?

...

WILL...

CAN YOU JUST STOP STARING AT ME?

YOU'RE GETTING ON MY NERVES. IF YOU DON'T STOP, I'LL KICK YOUR ASS.

THIS IS NOT ACCEPTABLE!

MONICA!!

...

YOU CAN'T KILL MRS. WYTTE!

SHE'S DAMIEN'S MUM! AND DORIAN'S AND DANIELA'S! IF YOU LOVE THEM, YOU CAN'T DO THIS!

WELL, IT'S NOT JUST MY CHOICE TO MAKE.

REMEMBER YOU ARE THE KING NOW.

WELL, THEN... I FORBID YOU!

WILLIAM... DROP IT.

THAT'S NOT HOW YOU FIX THINGS.

LOOK.

DON'T ASSUME I'VE SPENT YEARS STUDYING, RESEARCHING, AND IMPROVING...

... JUST TO MAKE A SLIGHTLY STRONGER HEALING POTION.

NO...

I'VE STILL GOT MANY ACES UP MY SLEEVE.

WHAT ARE YOU GONNA DO WITH THAT?

WHAT'S THAT POTION FOR?

MONICA!

...

TAKE IT.

YES, YOUR MAJESTY.

YOU ALREADY KNOW WHAT TO DO WITH IT.

BE DISCREET.

AT YOUR SERVICE, YOUR MAJESTY.

WE'RE HERE...

LAST TIME I WAS HERE FEELS LIKE YESTERDAY!

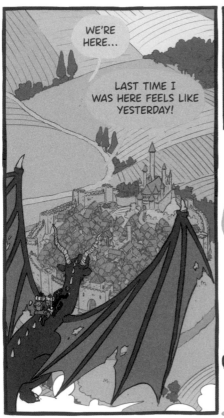

ONE SECOND, MARK, I NEED TO PUT THE LITTLE ONE IN MY BACKPACK!

HE COULD SCARE SOMEBODY IF THEY SEE HIM...

YOU SHOULD NAME HIM! GIVE HIM A POWERFUL NAME! LIKE BLOODY OR MONSTROUS...

COME ON, GET IN! BE GOOD. LOOK HOW CARLO'S HIDING!

YES, NICO TOO! I'M SURE THEY'D BE SCARED OF HIS FIERCENESS IF THEY SAW HIM...

THAT'S ENOUGH, IDIOT! I'D LIKE TO SEE YOU WITH MY SIZE!!

DEATH WING...

DEVIL...

TORMENT OF HEAVENS...

I WOULDN'T BE AS CUTE AS YOU, THAT'S FOR SURE.

BREATH OF HELL...

WOW... EVERYTHING'S BASICALLY THE SAME...

EVEN THOUGH IT'S CLEAR THAT DANI'S ARMY HASN'T CONQUERED THESE LANDS YET...

PEOPLE SEEM VERY QUIET.

UH...

IT WAS HERE...

THE PLACE WHERE THEY WERE GONNA KILL ME FOR WITCHCRAFT...

WHERE I SAW MONICA FOR THE LAST TIME...

WHERE DANI THOUGHT I...

IT'S WEIRD TO KNOW SO MUCH TIME HAS PASSED...

YOU'RE GONNA DIE, FOOLISH!

I'LL AVENGE MY SISTERS WHO DIED AT THE STAKE!!

NOOO, HELP!

HUH...

WHAT?!

...

WHAT A GAME...

MUAHAHA! YOU CAN'T RUN AWAY!

GET READY TO SUFFER MY WICKED MAGIC!

STOP, YOU EVIL WITCH!

OOOOH!

YES, IT'S ACTUALLY ME!! QUEEN MONICA, THE GOOD WITCH!! I'VE COME TO RESCUE YOU!!

I'M A GOOD WITCH TOO, LOOK! I'VE GOT A WAND!

THANK YOU, QUEEN MONICA!

YOUR POSH MAGIC CAN'T DEFEAT ME, LITTLE PRINCESS!

I'M NOT A PRINCESS, I'M A QUEEN!

AND YOU FELL INTO MY TRAP!! COME ON, SERVANTS, THROW THE POTION AT HER!

NOOOO!

HA-HA!

DORIAN? WHAT ARE YOU DOING?!

COME ON!

AH, SORRY!

I'M COMING!

ACCORDING TO THE LOCALS, DANI WAS HERE.

YES, AND SHE DESTROYED THE CATHEDRAL!

THAT'S SCARY...

IT SEEMS THAT I ALWAYS ARRIVE TOO LATE.

DON'T FEEL DISCOURAGED, MAN. WE HAD TO TRY IT!

I TOLD YOU DANI WOULD BE AT THE WEDDING!

WHOA! WHAT'S GOING ON?!

WITCHCRAFT!

THEY'RE SPIES OF QUEEN DANI!

WHAT THE...?!

WOOOW!

AHA! NOW YOU CAN FINALLY SEE MY REAL HEIGHT!

YOU'RE GOING TO BITE THE DUST, MARK! SEE WHO'S TALLER NOW!

...I DON'T WANT TO HEAR A WORD.

...

ANYWAY, THIS MUST MEAN THAT DANI IS HERE SOMEWHERE.

I ALWAYS GO BACK TO MY NORMAL SIZE WHEN SHE'S AROUND.

EH?

IT'S ME, DORIAN.

HUH, YES...

HIS VOICE.

IT SOUNDS SO DEEP!

BUT YES, IT'S REALLY HIM.

I'M SO SORRY...ABOUT DISAPPEARING FOR SO LONG.

I... MMMH...

THERE'S NO DOUBT.

THIS IS SO WEIRD...

I'VE DREAMT OF THIS MOMENT FOR SO LONG.

I JUST WANT TO HUG HIM AGAIN,

I WANNA CHECK IF HE'S TRULY ALIVE.

BUT...

WOULD THAT BE OK? HUGGING THIS PERSON?

117

HE LOOKS SO DIFFERENT. I FEEL WEIRD.

THIS...

THIS IS NOT WHAT I WAS EXPECTING...

UH... MONICA...

I WONDER WHAT IT FEELS LIKE TO HUG HIM.

ARE YOU ANGRY?

EH? NO, OF COURSE N...!

MONICA, LOOK!! THE SPELL SUDDENLY BROKE!!

NICO!! YOU'RE SO HANDSOME AND SUPER TALL!

I AM, AM I NOT?

OH, I'M SO GLAD!

HOW DID YOU GO BACK TO NORMAL?!

THAT'S WHY WE WERE WONDERING IF YOU HAD CAPTURED DANI OR...

I DON'T REALLY KNOW. I DIDN'T DO ANYTHING!

IF YOU HAD HEALED HER OR SOMETHING.

HI, MONICA!

ACTUALLY NO. DANI RAN AWAY BEFORE I COULD DO ANYTHING...

I DON'T KNOW WHERE SHE IS...

AW, HELLO SWEET CARLO! LONG TIME NO SEE!

...

I KNEW IT.

SHE HATES ME.

WE NEED TO GET THIS OVER WITH ONCE AND FOR ALL!

UH... YOU'RE RIGHT.

LET'S SAVE HER.

WHAT A CLICHÉ.

THIS IS MY CHANCE TO GET OUT OF HERE.

BUT WITHOUT MY WAND, THOUGH...

MMH?

OH, COME ON...

CLICK

THEY'RE SO USELESS. I COULD GET RID OF THEM ONCE AND FOR ALL, IF I WANTED TO.

IT'S TOO MUCH OF A MESS, THOUGH.

I'D BETTER NOT MAKE THINGS MORE COMPLICATED.

UH...

ALL RIGHT...

PERFECT.

BUT FIRST...

I NEED TO FIND DANI!

WHERE COULD SHE BE?

I THINK I'LL PAY A VISIT TO QUEEN MONICA...

129

131

I'M SO GLAD WE'RE TOGETHER AGAIN.

MUM... TONIGHT YOU'LL SLEEP IN MY ROOM.

DON'T TRY ANYTHING FUNNY. THE GUARDS WILL ESCORT US.

... FINE.

...

AH! OF COURSE!

NOW I KNOW WHY DANI'S CURSE BROKE TODAY!

DO YOU?

DANI CURSED ME A LONG TIME AGO IN ORDER TO PROTECT ME FROM HER MOTHER!

NOW THAT SHE HAS LOST HER POWERS, I'M NO LONGER IN DANGER!

WHAT DID YOU CALL ME?

HOW UNBELIEVABLY SMART OF YOU, NICO!

WHAT DO YOU MEAN, UNBELIEVABLY?!

133

WHERE DID MONICA GO?

SHE WAS A BIT WEIRD...

MONICA...?

WHAT'S WRONG?!

ARE YOU ALL RIGHT?!

DORIAN...!

YOU'RE SO PALE! ARE YOU FEELING DIZZY?

I'M FINE, I'M FINE!

BUT...!

DON'T TOUCH ME!

135

AS SOON AS I FIND DANI, WE'LL REBUILD EVERYTHING TOGETHER.

PHEW...

OH... ARE YOU FEELING BETTER?

YES... WAY BETTER.

AH, UM... SORRY FOR HUGGING YOU LIKE THAT.

I SAW YOU WERE VERY NERVOUS, AND I THOUGHT YOU WERE HAVING A PANIC ATTACK.

YES...

THANK YOU SO MUCH, DORIAN.

PLEASE... LET ME STAY LIKE THIS FOR A FEW MOMENTS.

...

I DON'T THINK WILLIAM WILL BE HAPPY ABOUT IT.

I'M TIRED, DAD! AND I'M HUNGRY! LET'S GO HOME AND EAT MAMA'S SOUP!

PATIENCE, ROBERT!

TOMORROW I'LL GO TO THE VILLAGE, AND I'M SURE PLENTY OF PEOPLE WILL WANT TO BUY A LOT OF FIREWOOD!

IT SEEMS THAT THE COLD WEATHER IS GONNA COME BACK IN THE NEXT COUPLE OF DAYS.

WELL, THAT'S WHY! IT'S SO COLD. WE SHOULD BE AT HOME DRINKING HOT SOUP!

UGH!

DADDY?! WHY HAVE YOU STOPPED ALL OF A SUDDEN?!

THERE'S...

THERE'S SOMEONE IN THE DARK...

AH, THAT'S TRUE...

IT'S A GIRL!

GOOD EVENING, LADY! ARE YOU ALL RIGHT?!

COME TO OUR SHELTER! WE'VE GOT HOT SOUP!

AND LOTS OF FIREWOOD!

AND WHERE COULD WE FIND THE LUMBERJACK, GUYS?

DO YOU BELIEVE WHAT THEY'RE SAYING?

WHAT ARE YOU DOING, AISHA?

IT'S THE ONLY CLUE THAT WE'VE GOT AT THE MOMENT.

DID YOU HEAR THAT, MONICA? DANI IS EATING KIDS NOW.

CAN YOU PLEASE STOP STARING AND POINTING AT THEM, WILLIAM?

WE'RE SUPPOSED TO GO UNNOTICED.

...

HEY, DORIAN...

I'VE ALSO SEEN HER WITH RED EYES, AND IT CLEARLY WASN'T HER.

SHE WAS SORT OF POSSESSED.

THE REAL DANI'S STILL THERE AND WE CAN SAVE HER.

YOU HEARD THAT, RIGHT? DANI IS IN THE MOUNTAINS.

YES...

BUT IF THEY'RE ALREADY SCARED OF WITCHES, FLYING UP THERE WOULD BE DANGEROUS.

HOW CAN WE GET THERE WITHOUT BEING SEEN?

LEAVE IT TO ME AND MARK.

♪♪♪

♫

AW! YOU LOOK SO HAPPY, MONICA!

I HAVEN'T HEARD YOU SING IN A WHILE!

INDEED, THREE YEARS TO BE PRECISE.

IT MUST BE THE HAPPINESS OF THE NEWLY MARRIED!

YEEEAH, SURE THING...

UGH!

HEY, DORIAN. ARE YOU OK, DUDE?

...

I'M SCARED...

DO YOU WANNA SEE SOMETHING REALLY COOL?

OH! A CRYSTAL BALL!

I GOT IT FROM MONICA'S SECRET LABORATORY!

DO YOU WANT ME TO TRY TO SEE THE FUTURE...?

EH, BLOODY! DON'T BE SO SELFISH AND LEAVE SOME FOOD FOR CARLO!

BAD DRAGON, BAD DRAGON!

BLOODY? HIS NAME IS NOT BLOODY!

HMM?

HAVE YOU ALREADY GIVEN HIM A NAME?

YES! HIS NAME IS DONATO!

DONATO THE DRAGON!

DORIAN, THAT'S NOT A DRAGON NAME AT ALL!

EH? WELL, I THINK IT SUITS HIM... BESIDES, HE LIKES IT. ISN'T THAT RIGHT, DONATO?

THAT'S TRUE, HE LIKES IT.

HUFF...

HA...

I'M SO TIRED...

HOW LONG HAVE WE BEEN CLIMBING?

144

I TOLD YOU IT WAS GONNA RAIN!

AND WHAT DID YOU EXPECT US TO DO?!

WE HAD TO CLIMB THE MOUNTAIN!

IF ONLY DORIAN WASN'T SO SLOW!

I DO... WHAT I CAN.

STOP FIGHTING! WE NEED TO TAKE COVER!

AH!

LOOK, OVER THERE! IT'S THE LUMBERJACK'S SHELTER!

WE'VE ARRIVED!

HUH... BUT... LOOK AT THE WINDOWS...

IT SEEMS LIKE SOMETHING MUST HAVE SCARED THEM A LOT...

YEAH...

GOOD NEWS, THEN.

DANI IS HERE SOMEWHERE.

KNOCK KNOCK KNOCK

145

ME
TOO.

SOB
SOB

GUYS,
GET INSIDE! LET'S
HAVE DINNER!

AND SHUT
THE DOOR, OR
THE COLD GETS
IN.

YES! I'M
SORRY, MADAM!

THANK YOU SO
MUCH! IT SMELLS
SO GOOD!

YEAH, WELL...
ABOUT WHAT YOU
WERE ASKING,
GUYS...

IT'S TRUE,
WE SAW A WITCH
IN THE MIDDLE OF
THE MOUNTAIN, AT
NIGHT...

149

LOOK! I'VE GOT A CRYSTAL BALL!

I HAVEN'T USED IT IN A LONG TIME. I HOPE IT'LL WORK! COME ON, SHOW ME HOW WE'RE GONNA RESCUE DANI!

AH... I CAN SEE SOMETHING...

WOOO!! WHAT DO YOU SEE?!

AWESOME!

GOOD IDEA, NICO!

EH?

IT SHOWED DORIAN WITH A PAIR OF SHORTS!!

WHAT A CRAPPY CRYSTAL BALL!!

EH?

REALLY?! IN SHORTS?!

PERHAPS THE BALL IS SUGGESTING THAT WE'LL SAVE DANI IN SUMMER?

WELL, IT'S DECEMBER NOW, SO...

SHORTS...

HOW WEIRD...

YAWN

COME ON, GET IN BED, EVERYONE! YOU MUST BE EXHAUSTED!

YOU CAN SLEEP IN THE BUNK BEDS!

THANK YOU SO MUCH!

WOULD IT BE POSSIBLE TO HAVE A PRIVATE ROOM FOR MY WIFE AND I? WE'RE NEWLY WED, YOU KNOW...?

AH...!

151

WELL, I MEAN THAT... I DON'T KNOW... MAYBE WE SHOULD ANNUL THE MARRIAGE...

SOMEHOW...?

WE CAN'T DO THAT! OUR DUTY HAS ALWAYS BEEN THE UNION OF OUR KINGDOMS!

I WAS RAISED FOR THAT!!

WE CAN'T SPLIT UP NOW. THE PEOPLE WOULDN'T ACCEPT IT. IT'D BE A DISASTER!

WELL, THEN... I DON'T KNOW, I...

CAN'T WE SIMPLY PRETEND?

WH...?

WE'LL BE THE KING AND THE QUEEN THAT THEY ALL NEED!

BUT IT'S NOBODY'S BUSINESS IF WE'RE TOGETHER IN PRIVATE.

WHAT YOU'RE SAYING DOESN'T MAKE ANY SENSE.

... WITH DORIAN...? THAT BRAT...?

!

WILLIAM, WAIT!

UH... I'M IN LOVE WITH HIM!

I'M...!

AND I...

I WANT...

...

UH... WHAT DID I JUST SAY?

TO ANNUL THE MARRIAGE?

SHE'S IN LOVE WITH DORIAN?

IN LOVE?!

WHEN DID THAT HAPPEN?!

WHAT THE HELL IS WRONG WITH MONICA?!

CAN'T SHE UNDERSTAND THAT SHE'S THE QUEEN?!

WE NEED TO FULFILL OUR OBLIGATIONS!

THAT'S WHAT OUR PARENTS TOLD US!!

THAT'S WHAT THE WHOLE KINGDOM IS EXPECTING OF US!

WHY DOES SHE WANT TO THROW IT ALL AWAY...?!

WHY?!

ONLY BECAUSE SHE WANTS TO BE WITH DORIAN?

I DON'T GET IT.

WHAT DO YOU WANT, WILL?

IT'S MY DUTY TO MARRY MONICA.

TO BE HER HUSBAND.

TO BE THE KING.

WHAT'S ON YOUR MIND?

WHAT DO YOU WANT?

...

WOW... IT LOOKS LIKE THERE'S PLENTY OF PEOPLE IN THIS HOUSE...

GOOD...

KILL THEM.

LET ONLY ONE LIVE.

IT'LL BE GOOD...

...

ALL RIGHT.

DANI!

IT'S ME, DORIAN!

DANI, SAY SOMETHING!

WHAT'S GOING ON?

WHY ARE YOU BEING SO LOUD?!

IT'S YOUR SISTER!!

WHAT?!

DORIAN...

I THINK SHE...

SHE CAN'T RECOGNIZE ME...

I DON'T KNOW WHAT SORT OF REACTION I WAS EXPECTING FROM HER, BUT...

SHE ISN'T RESPONDING AT ALL.

165

169

172

DANI, LOOK AT ME!

IT'S ME, DORIAN!

I'M YOUR BROTHER!

LOOK CLOSELY, WE LOOK A LOT LIKE EACH OTHER!

... BROTHER?

YES, IT'S ME!

DO YOU REMEMBER ME NOW?!

UGH...

COME ON, GET UP. I WILL TAKE YOU TO THE OTHERS.

TOGETHER, WE WILL FIND A WAY FOR YOU TO GET BETTER.

174

NO...

I WON'T LET YOU TAKE HER AWAY...

WHEW, YOU'VE ALSO GROWN UP A LOT! YOU'RE AS TALL AS NICO! OR MAYBE A BIT MORE...?

UH...

DANI?

HUH?

WHAT ARE YOU DOING?!

DA...!

WHAT IS GOING ON?!

...NI...

UH...

RED EYES.

FOCUS, DORIAN.

WHAT HAVE YOU READ ABOUT RED EYES?

182

AAARGH!

I SAID A MOUSE!

IT WAS SUPPOSED TO BE A NORMAL-SIZED SNAKE!

...GIANT SNAKE?!

WHY IS IT SO BIG?! I DON'T GET IT!

TURN IT INTO DANI AGAIN, QUICK!

YES, RIGHT AWAY!

BUT FIRST...

RUN!

WAAAAAH!

WHOA... COOL...

WELL, YEAH... HE'S QUITE IMPRESSIVE...

THANK YOU SO MUCH, DAMIEN! YOU RULE!

COME ON, YOU GUYS! THE OTHERS NEED OUR HELP!

WHY DID WILLIAM LOOK AT ME THAT WAY? WHAT IS THAT IDIOT THINKING?

AAAARGH, I'M THE REAL IDIOT HERE. I'M WAY TOO HAPPY.

NO, NO, NO, DAMIEN. NOW IS NOT THE TIME.

YOUR CLUMSY SIBLINGS NEED TO BE RESCUED BEFORE THEY GET HURT FOR REAL.

KEEP A CLEAR HEAD!

TAKE IT, DAMIEN!

AH!

HURRY UP, WILL! GET ON MY BROOM!

DON'T WORRY, I'LL GET ON DAMIEN'S BROOM. IT'S NOT THE FIRST TIME HE'S TAKEN ME AS A COPILOT!

CLEAR HEAD. CLEAR HEAD.

!

WHILE WE'RE FLYING YOU CAN GIVE ME LOVE ADVICE, DAMIEN.

NOW THAT I'M SINGLE AGAIN.

IF YOU DON'T SHUT UP, I'LL THROW YOU OFF THE BROOM, YOU FOOL.

DAMIEN. I WANT TO TELL YOU SOMETHING BEFORE WE CONFRONT DANI AGAIN.

I BROUGHT THIS TO USE IN CASE IT IS NECESSARY.

IT'S... THE POTION I USED ON YOUR MOTHER, YES.

TO END HER MAGICAL POWERS FOREVER.

I CAN THROW IT AWAY IF YOU WANT. I'M NOT SURE IF I WAS RIGHT TO BRING IT.

NO, KEEP IT.

JUST IN CASE.

200

UGH...

THIS STUPID BODY ONCE AGAIN...

I NEED TO GAIN STRENGTH...OR THAT SPOILED BRAT WON'T LET ME USE HERS...

AH! YOU FINALLY APPEARED!

ABOUT TIME!

HAVEN'T YOU NOTICED?!

?

LOOK, KILL THEM ALL AND LET'S GET OUT OF HERE.

I WAS DOING SO WELL, BEING A GIANT SNAKE...

HEY... THEY'RE AFTER YOU!

I'M BORED OUT OF MY HEAD. THESE PEOPLE ARE TIRING.

... ALL RIGHT.

DANI...

AH! LOOK! DORIAN'S OVER THERE!

SHE SAW US!

TRUE. I HOPE HE'S FIN--

UGH!

208

AH... I THINK... I THINK I'VE BEEN HERE BEFORE.

HUH?

THE SHELTER... WHEN DID WE RETURN?

WHAT...? WHAT WAS I DOING OUT THERE?

I FEEL LIKE I JUST WOKE UP FROM A DREAM...

DO YOU THINK DORIAN WILL COME BACK?

BAH, WHO CARES!

!

WITH A BIT OF LUCK HE AND DANI WILL KILL EACH OTHER!

HAHAHA, DAMN, NICO, YOU'RE SO MEAN!

ARE THEY TALKING ABOUT ME...?

YOU KNOW THOSE TWO HAVEN'T GIVEN US ANYTHING BUT PROBLEMS SINCE THEIR ARRIVAL.

IT SEEMS LIKE THEY ARE CURSED!

I THINK THEY ARE INDEED!

HOW SICK.

AND ON TOP OF THAT, DORIAN IS SUCH A PAIN. I NEVER LIKED HIM ANYWAY.

DANI WAS SO COOL. IT'S SUCH A SHAME THAT SHE WENT CRAZY!

WHATEVER, THERE'S NOTHING TO DO!

YES, IT LOOKS LIKE EVERYTHING'S GOING GREAT. WE'VE KILLED TWO BIRDS WITH ONE STONE AND WITHOUT GETTING OUR HANDS DIRTY.

I WANT TO GO BACK TO THE PALACE. I NEVER THOUGHT MY FAMILY WOULD PERSECUTE ME FOR SO LONG! WHAT A NIGHTMARE!

THERE'S A REASON WHY I GOT OUT OF THERE.

YEAH, IT MUST BE HARD TO BE BLOOD BOUND TO SUCH TWISTED PEOPLE.

SLAM

AH, DORIAN...

DORIAN! WHAT ARE YOU DOING HERE?

DID YOU ACTUALLY HEAR...?

THIS IS STUPID. IT MAKES NO SENSE.

I DON'T KNOW WHO YOU ARE, BUT YOU'RE NOT MY FRIENDS.

HMM... I'D SAY THIS DOOR WASN'T HERE BEFORE...

WHERE ARE YOU GOING, DORIAN?

I'M LOOKING FOR DANI.

SOMETHING TELLS ME SHE'S REALLY CLOSE...

... WHO'S THAT?

HMM...?

AH... YOU.

HI, SON.

IT'S BEEN A LONG TIME.

I'M GLAD TO SEE YOU'VE GROWN UP...

YOU RESEMBLE ME A LOT!

EVEN THOUGH I WOULD NEVER HAVE BETRAYED MY OWN FAMILY TO THE POINT OF KILLING MY FATHER.

YOU'VE GOT SOME AUDACITY, DORIAN...

IN THE END, YOU'RE THE MOST TWISTED AMONG US...

HUH?

I'VE GOT NO TIME FOR SUCH SILLINESS.

I KNOW YOU'RE NOT MY REAL FATHER, AND ALL OF THIS SOUNDS LIKE A BAD JOKE.

I NEED TO FIND DANI. LEAVE ME ALONE.

WHERE DO YOU THINK YOU'RE GOING?! MURDERER!

YOU'VE KILLED ME! YOU'LL NEVER FIND DANI!

HEY...

HELLO, SWEETHEART...

STOP IT, SERIOUSLY. THE MORE YOU TRY, THE MORE I REMEMBER THIS PLACE.

IT'S NOT THE FIRST TIME YOU TRIED TO SCARE ME.

215

EVERYTHING... EVERYTHING'S GOING WRONG, DORIAN. WE NEED TO FIX THIS!

DON'T WORRY, DANI. EVERYTHING'S GONNA BE OK NOW.

NOW THAT I'VE FOUND YOU.

I'VE BEEN LOOKING FOR YOU FOR SO LONG.

THIS PLACE IS SO COLD AND LONELY...

IS THIS HOW YOU FEEL, DANI?

HAVE YOU BEEN ON YOUR OWN, LOCKED UP IN HERE ALL THIS TIME?

DORIAN... I'M SO SORRY...

I'M GLAD YOU'RE HERE.

YOU'LL STAY WITH ME NOW. AND I WON'T BE ALONE ANYMORE!

HUH?

STAY?

NOTHING IS. DANI'S NOT HERE. YOU TOOK MY BIGGEST WISH TO USE IT AGAINST ME!

I THOUGHT YOUR FIRST ATTEMPTS TO SCARE ME OFF WERE CLUMSY,

BUT YOU WERE ONLY TRYING TO FOOL ME INTO THINKING THAT YOU DIDN'T WANT ME TO SEE DANI!

DANI HAS NEVER BEEN HERE IN THE FIRST PLACE!

WHAT ARE YOU SAYING, DORIAN?

IT'S REALLY ME. I'M DANI!

WHO ELSE COULD I BE?

THE CAT!

WHO?

AH!

IT'S TRYING TO POSSESS ME!

AH!

THE WAND!

I HAVE TO...!

UGH...

GOOD...

DORIAN...?

YOUR EYES...!

NO...! DON'T TELL ME THAT YOU ARE...?

NO.

I'M OKAY.

221

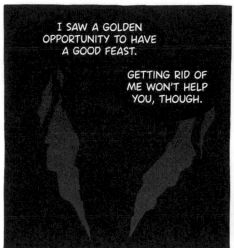

I SAW A GOLDEN OPPORTUNITY TO HAVE A GOOD FEAST.

GETTING RID OF ME WON'T HELP YOU, THOUGH.

THERE'S SOMETHING WAY MORE POWERFUL...

YOUR SISTER ISN'T COMING BACK.

YOU LEARNED HOW TO DO THAT BY READING THOSE CREEPY NOTES?

DORIAN, DUDE, THAT WAS IMPRESSIVE!

WHOA...

WHAT...? WHAT HAPPENED?

I THINK WE FELL ASLEEP.

I JUST HAD THE WEIRDEST DREAM...

MY CUPCAKES WERE BURNING THE ENTIRE TIME.

DANI...?

UH...

WHAT DO I LOOK LIKE?

SUPER HANDSOME.

COOL!

DANI... ARE YOU OK?

HOW ARE YOU FEELING?

CAN YOU REMEMBER ME?

...

... NO.

WHAT ABOUT ME? REMEMBER ME?

YES, NICO.

CAN YOU REMEMBER HOW WE MET?

... YOU WERE...IN THE DARK CASTLE.

...

WHAT ABOUT EVERYONE ELSE? CAN YOU REMEMBER ALL THESE PEOPLE?

... NO.

DAMIEN... WHAT'S GOING ON? WHY DIDN'T IT WORK?

I DON'T KNOW.

DORIAN SUPPOSEDLY GOT RID OF THE EVIL SPIRIT THAT WAS POSSESSING HER, BUT...

DANI... TELL ME, WOULD YOU LIKE TO COME TO THE SHELTER WITH US?

ALL RIGHT.

GOOD...

COME ON, STAND UP!

IF IT'S HARD FOR YOU TO WALK, I'LL CARRY YOU!

YOU KNOW I CAN HANDLE YOUR WEIGHT. I'M STRONG NOW.

I CAN WALK.

OKAY... IT SEEMS LIKE SHE IS NO LONGER AGGRESSIVE NOW THAT THE SPIRIT IS GONE...

LET'S TAKE HER TO THE SHELTER.

WE ALL NEED SOME SLEEP. I'M PRETTY SURE WE STINK.

AND A GOOD SHOWER!

WE'LL TAKE CARE OF DANI THERE. COME ON!

UGH...

AH... DORIAN?

I...I'M SORRY!

I CAN'T... UGH...

HEY...

!

DORIAN, WAIT!

WHERE ARE YOU GOING?!

UUUGH...

UGH...

DORIAN...

HEY...

SHE DOESN'T REMEMBER, MONICA! SHE DOESN'T REMEMBER ME!

I THOUGHT I COULD SAVE HER...

BUT I COULDN'T DO ANYTHING.

OF COURSE YOU DID! SHE'S WITH US NOW.

SHE'S NOT! THAT'S NOT DANI!

SHE'S SAFE!

WE CAN BRING HER BACK, DORIAN. WE'LL HEAL HER. ALL OF US.

WE'LL FIGURE OUT WHAT HAPPENED AND FIND A SOLUTION.

YOU DON'T GET IT, MONICA...

THE SPIRIT... BEFORE IT DISAPPEARED, IT TOLD ME...

IT TOLD ME DANI WASN'T COMING BACK, THAT SOMETHING POWERFUL WAS HOLDING HER BACK...

AND ARE YOU GONNA TRUST AN EVIL SPIRIT?

IT FED ON PAIN, REMEMBER?

IT JUST WANTED TO HURT YOU.

...

UH... BUT HOW'S IT POSSIBLE...

THAT SHE DOESN'T REMEMBER ME?

MONICA...

I'M TIRED.

TONIGHT... DAMN, IT WAS SCARY.

YES...

AND YOU DIDN'T SEE THE GIANT SNAKE!

I PROMISE WE'LL FIND A SOLUTION.

TOGETHER.

UH...

THANK YOU...

FOR EVERYTHING.

SERIOUSLY, I...

AH...

I...

UH...

ARE YOU FEELING BETTER?

YES.

DO YOU WANT TO JOIN THE OTHERS?

NO.

WELL, IT'S NOT REALLY YOUR FAULT...

IT WAS ACTUALLY THE WITCH WHO DID IT...

EVEN THOUGH SHE DOESN'T LOOK DANGEROUS NOW.

JUST A BIT STUNNED.

IS SHE OK?

YES, MADAM, SHE'S STILL IN SHOCK.

WHY DID YOU BRING HER HERE?

SHE'S GONNA EAT US ALL!

DANI ISN'T GONNA HURT ANYONE.

WE'VE SAID IT BEFORE, SHE WAS POSSESSED BY AN EVIL SPIRIT.

HOW CAN YOU BE SO SURE, THOUGH? HOW DID YOU GET RID OF THE SPIRIT?

WHAT?

USING MAGIC, OF COURSE!

THAT'S WHAT MAGIC IS FOR!

THERE'S NOTHING IN THAT IMAGE APART FROM DANI, AND THAT WRETCHED CAT AND I!

AND THE CAT ISN'T A PROBLEM ANYMORE...

I'M OVERLOOKING SOMETHING HERE.

BUT WHAT?

DANI...

I'D BETTER DISCUSS THIS WITH THE OTHERS. MAYBE TOGETHER WE'LL DISCOVER SOMETHING...

AH...

UH...
WHAT TIME IS IT...?

DID I FALL ASLEEP...?

AH, DORIAN!

OH MY, OH MY.

WAAAAAA!

MONICA, I HAD A GREAT IDEA!

I KNOW HOW TO MAKE DANI REMEMBER ME.

I'VE GOT A BRILLIANT PLAN.

A PLAN?

YES! COME ON, STAND UP! WE NEED TO EXPLAIN MY PLAN TO EVERYONE!

COMING!

238

STOP COMPLAINING, AMIR. YOU HAVEN'T DONE ANYTHING USEFUL UNTIL NOW!

YOU'RE THE FEARLESS ONE, AISHA!

I'M NOT GOOD AT ANYTHING THAT IMPLIES MOVING FROM THE DIVAN, YOU KNOW THAT.

I GET THIS FROM MOTHER.

I CAN HEAR YOU.

SHUT UP AND COME. YOU'RE SO LAZY!

AISHA, YOU'VE JUST COME BACK AND YOU'RE LEAVING AGAIN?

MONICA NEEDS US!

TURNS OUT WE'LL BE SAVING THE DAY IN THE END.

DORIAN HAS A PLAN!

WE'LL GIVE DANI HER MEMORY BACK, AND WE NEED PEOPLE WHO KNEW HER THREE YEARS AGO!

SO COME ON, THERE'S NO TIME TO LOSE!

240

HELLO, PRINCESS MONICA! OH...YOUR MAJESTY, NOW? IT'S BEEN SO LONG!

HI, MR. EVANS! IS EVERYTHING ALL RIGHT?

YES, SHE'S TAKING A BATH.

DID YOU BRING HER CLOTHES?

YES... BUT LOOK AT THIS!

THIS IS UNACCEPTABLE!

THAT'S WHAT SHE WAS WEARING EARLIER, ISN'T IT?

YES! CAN YOU BELIEVE IT?!

DORIAN PERFORMED ONE OF THOSE SPELLS TO FIX THE DAMAGE, AND THAT'S IT!

I TOLD HIM DANI COULDN'T JUST GO AROUND DRESSED AS AN EVIL WITCH! NO WAY!

I EVEN OFFERED TO GO SHOPPING MYSELF!

SHOPPING...? IT SEEMS DIFFICULT, JUDGING BY THE STATE OF THE VILLAGE...

ALL BUSINESSES CLOSED WHEN THE WAR BROKE OUT.

THOUGH THERE IS A LADY WHO USED TO BE A DRESSMAKER...

THAT SOUNDS PERFECT!

ARE YOU GONNA DESIGN IT? CAN YOU DRAW?

241

TALKING TO YOURSELF AGAIN?

I'M TALKING TO DONATO.

MONICA SAYS THAT YOU NEED MY INVALUABLE HELP.

OF COURSE! I'M THE KEY TO SOLVING THE MYSTERY WHICH HOLDS DANI CAPTIVE.

THANK YOU FOR FINDING NICO, DESPITE HOW STUBBORN I GOT OVER DANI'S CLOTHES.

...

HEY, ARE YOU LISTENING?

OH, YEAH, I'M SORRY.

THAT'S RIGHT, I NEED YOUR HELP.

WHAT DO WE NEED TO DO, THEN?

WE NEED TO REBUILD MASTER PENDRAGON'S HOUSE, JUST AS IT WAS BEFORE THE FLAMES DESTROYED IT.

WE NEED TO BE PRECISE, CAREFUL THAT EACH DETAIL IS EXACTLY LIKE OLD TIMES.

THAT'S WHY I NEED TO MAKE A REBUILDING PLAN BETWEEN US THREE.

YOU LIVED HERE LONGER THAN ANYONE ELSE, NICO, SO I TRUST YOUR MEMORY.

CONSIDER IT DONE.

KING WILLIAM WENT LOOKING FOR BRICKS, STONE, WOOD...

MATERIALS THAT WE NEED TO RECONSTRUCT THE HOUSE.

IN THE MEANTIME, I SENT DAMIEN TO LOOK FOR A WAND, SINCE MINE BROKE.

I TOLD HIM TO BORROW IT FROM A NEIGHBOR.

MANY WITCHES LIVE IN THE AREA NOW; MAYBE SOMEONE WILL HELP US.

WHEN I WOKE UP AFTER THREE YEARS, I FELT VERY STRANGE.

EVERYTHING WAS DIFFERENT; WE HAD ALL GROWN UP ALL OF A SUDDEN.

PERHAPS THE SAME HAPPENED TO DANI.

MAYBE SHE DIDN'T RECOGNIZE ME 'CAUSE I'VE CHANGED TOO MUCH.

MAYBE IF WE MANAGE TO MAKE THIS WORLD RESEMBLE THE ONE SHE LOVED AND LEFT BEHIND...

MAYBE AT THAT POINT...

SHE'LL BE ABLE TO REMEMBER AND COME BACK.

SO, THE LAST PART OF THE PLAN, THE MOST IMPORTANT...

LEAVE IT TO ME, OF COURSE!

WHOAAAA, IMPRESSIVE.

IT'S BACK TO HOW IT WAS BEFORE THE FIRE!

PERFECT.

IT'S ALMOST READY...

HEY, NICO... LISTEN...

THANK YOU FOR SAYING THAT.

I STILL LOVE MY PARENTS. I WANT MY MUM TO REDEEM HERSELF AND REBOOT HER LIFE,

DESPITE THE FACT THAT THEY STARTED A GRUESOME WAR AND TRIED TO INVOLVE THEIR OWN CHILDREN.

AND THEY KILLED MY PARENTS.

THAT'S RIGHT, THEY KILLED MONICA'S PARENTS.

BUT YOU SHOULD STOP TORTURING YOURSELF.

THEY ALSO KILLED MANY NEIGHBORS IN THE VILLAGE, SOME OF MY FRIENDS' MOTHERS AND FATHERS, WHEN I WAS A LITTLE BOY.

IT WAS TRAUMATIZING.

AND BEFORE THAT, MY FATHER ORDERED YOUR MOTHER TO BE BURNED FOR SIMPLY BEING A WITCH.

I SUPPOSE HE'S TO BLAME FOR ALL OF THIS.

WELL, IN TRUTH, THE FIRST ONE WHO SENT HUNDREDS OF WITCHES TO THE STAKE WAS MY FATHER.

HE'S ALSO TO BE BLAMED...

MUM AND DAD SET ME AGAINST YOU. IT WAS ALL VERY CONFUSING AND...

NOW I DO SEE YOU'RE A GOOD PERSON, DAMIEN.

AND I'M NOT SCARED OF YOU ANYMORE.

YOU'RE THE ONLY OLDER BROTHER I'VE GOT, AND...

I'D LIKE FOR US TO REALLY BEHAVE LIKE BROTHERS FROM NOW ON.

DORIAN...

I'M SO SORRY I ABANDONED BOTH YOU AND DANI IN THAT HOUSE.

HUH?

I LEFT KNOWING THAT IT WAS A TOXIC PLACE. I LEFT YOU BEHIND.

I WAS A SCARED KID, AND...

AND I'M SELFISH. THAT'S THE TRUTH.

I'VE NEVER BEEN ABLE TO FORGIVE MYSELF.

I THOUGHT I WOULDN'T NEED TO FACE IT. I TRIED TO GET YOU OUT OF MY HEAD, PRETEND YOU DIDN'T EXIST.

BUT YOU'RE HERE NOW, SAYING THAT YOU WANNA FIX THINGS.

INCLUDING OUR FAMILY.

OF COURSE. IT'S ALL GETTING FIXED.

...

SHE LOOKS QUITE HARMLESS WHEN SHE'S ASLEEP.

AISHA! WHEN DID YOU ARRIVE?

A FEW HOURS AGO.

THE OTHERS ARE DOWNSTAIRS, EMPTYING YOUR FATHER'S CUPBOARD.

ARE... ARE YOU SURE WE'RE ALLOWED TO EAT ALL THESE CAKES?

IF ANYONE ASKS YOU, JUST SAY YOU HAVEN'T SEEN ANYTHING.

WE'VE BEEN HAVING DINNER AT THE MASTER'S HOUSE.

YOU SHOULD HAVE COME, AISHA!

YEAH, YOUR FATHER TOLD ME...

I DON'T KNOW. I DIDN'T WANT TO BOTHER YOU BY JOINING THE GROUP WITHOUT WARNING...

AH...

SO CUUUTE!

HEY!

YOU WERE WEARING THOSE SHORTS THE FIRST TIME I SAW YOU. REMEMBER?

I USED TO CALL YOU FROG-KID!

YES... AND I TRIED TO IMPRESS YOU... HOW PATHETIC.

OH, BUT YOU IMPRESSED AND ALSO SCARED ME.

I NOTICED I EARNED YOUR ADMIRATION WHEN YOU STOPPED CALLING ME FROG-KID,

AND YOU STARTED CALLING ME PROFESSOR WYTTE.

AAAAAH! WHAT ARE YOU TALKING ABOUT!

YOU'RE NOT CUTE ANYMORE!

HEY, YOU TWO!

MAKE SURE TO OPEN THE DOOR FROM THE FLOOR, MAJESTY!

YES!

AND CRYING! CRYING IS VERY IMPORTANT!

DING DONG

DING DONG

DING DONG

SHE'S HERE!

COMING! WAIT A MINUTE!

SEE YOU SOON!

DING DONG

GOOD LUCK!

DING DONG

OH, HI CARLO!

DO YOU KNOW YOUR LINES, BUDDY?

AH... HELLO...

YOU'RE FINALLY HERE!

WELCOME!

...

COME ON IN, COME ON IN.

YOUR BROTHER'S WAITING FOR YOU INSIDE.

HERE, HAVE A SEAT, YOUNG LADY.

GREAT.

I'M GONNA MAKE YOU SOME HOT CHOCOLATE NOW, KIDS.

AHEM...

WHAT A MESS, HUH DANI?

IT WAS SUCH BAD LUCK, MISSING OUR SCHOOL BUS LIKE THAT!

WE'RE HOPELESS!

... BUS?

THERE YOU GO, KIDS.

THANKS.

UH...

PRINCE WILLIAM, REMEMBER YOUR LINE: "I ACCEPT YOU BOTH AS..."

OH, RIGHT!

CHILDREN, I ACCEPT YOU BOTH AS APPRENTICES...

TO FIGHT AGAINST THE EVIL WITCHES!

COOL!

...

SLURP

DING DONG

OPEN THE DOOR, MASTER!

PRINCESS MONICA'S HERE TO TALK TO YOU!

WELCOME, MY DEAR PRINCESS MONICA!

HI THERE!

AH... HELLO...

LET ME INTRODUCE MYSELF.

I'M DORIAN, HEIR OF THE WYTTE FAMILY.

AH... WHAT A CUTE KID!

...

HI DANI!

HELLO, NICO.

WHAT'S GOING ON?

SINCE PRINCESS MONICA'S HERE, WE'LL NEED TO BE CAREFUL NOT TO DO MAGIC!

SHE HATES WITCHES!

WHOOSH

EH. EASY THERE!

YOU'RE STILL STUDENTS!

EXACTLY, GO STUDY!

?

WE NEED TO LEARN GOOD SPELLS!

UM... YES...

READ THE BOOK.

AND PRACTICE.

YES, THAT'S IT.

LOOK, DANI!

NOW I KNOW HOW TO MAKE ICE!

CAN YOU REMEMBER THIS SPELL?

DANI, LOOK AT MY TOY CASTLE!

IT'S JUST LIKE MY REAL HOME!

DANI. I'M GONNA KILL YOU.

CAN YOU REMEMBER THE LOVE POTION THAT WENT WRONG?

WELL, I HATE YOU NOW.

LOOK, THE LITTLE AIRPLANE YOU NEED TO STEAL FROM MARK!

IS IT WORKING?

SHUT UP, WILL! YOU'RE SUPPOSED TO BE ASLEEP.

HEY...

DOES THIS RING A BELL?

WHAT ABOUT THE BALL? CAN YOU REMEMBER?

YOU LOOKED SO CUTE! DRESSED IN BLUE!

DORIAN.

THIS IS NOT WORKING.

...

WAIT.

COME ON, DANI! LET'S GO UPSTAIRS!

CAN YOU REMEMBER THIS ROOM?

I USED TO SLEEP HERE,

AND YOU USED TO COME HERE WHEN YOU COULDN'T SLEEP.

THIS IS WHERE WE REHEARSE OUR DANCE STEPS!

LOOK AT THAT! DO YOU REMEMBER IT?

HEY, DANI.

WHAT?

ARE YOU UP FOR A RACE?

A RACE?

YES.

DON'T YOU ENJOY FLYING?

LET'S GO!

DON'T BE A COWARD, DANI!

WE'RE GONNA FLY ON A BROOM!

ALL RIGHT.

AWESOME!

YOU'RE GOING DOWN!

YOU'LL SEE HOW QUICK I AM, DANI!

277

OH NO!

SHE'S GONNA DROWN!

NICO, GET HER OUT OF THERE!

ARGH!

I NEED TO DO SOMETHING!

CARLO!

THERE YOU GO, DAMIEN.

DORIAN, TAKE THE BROOM.

NO, I WON'T BE OF ANY HELP WITH THAT.

I ACTUALLY NEED IT.

THANKS, DAMIEN.

IF ONLY I KNEW HOW TO USE A BOW...

AT LEAST I COULD HELP A LITTLE.

THROW SOME ROCKS AT THE MONSTER.

AISHA...

AS FAR AS I'M CONCERNED,

YOU'D BE AS USEFUL AS I AM, RIGHT NOW.

YOU'LL BE SORRY, YOU FOUL BEAST.

UH...

MY SPELL DIDN'T EVEN SCRATCH IT.

THEN LET'S SEE...

...IF YOU CAN DODGE MY BARRIER!

AT LEAST THIS WAY YOU'LL STAY STILL.

WHAT?!

HOW IS THIS POSSIBLE?!

DAMIEN'S SPELLS AREN'T WORKING...

THIS LOOKS BAD...

OUT OF THE WAY!

!

WAIT, MONICA! WHAT ARE YOU GONNA DO?

YOU CAN'T CAST SPELLS!

WAIT!

UGH!

IT SEEMS THAT DAMIEN'S SPELLS AREN'T HURTING THE MONSTER AT ALL!

NEITHER ARE THE ARROWS.

PERHAPS IF I FREEZE THE WATER SURROUNDING IT, IT'LL BE PARALYZED.

NO!

WE SHOULD ONLY ATTACK THE BEAST.

WE DON'T KNOW IF DANI'S STILL IN THE WATER!

SPELLS AND ARROWS AREN'T WORKING.

I HAVE TO DO SOMETHING.

FOR ONCE...

I HAVE TO BE USEFUL.

!

WH... WHAT...

WILL, YOU IDIOT, WHAT ARE YOU DOING?!

DON'T BE STUPID!

WILL...?

DAMIEN CAN'T GET ANGRY AT ME.

IT IS MY DUTY AS A KING TO PROTECT THEM ALL.

EVEN IF IT'S THE FIRST AND LAST TIME.

I'LL KILL YOU...

FROM INSIDE.

OH NO...!

THERE'S SOMETHING STRANGE HERE.

WE ATTACKED THE CREATURE WITH SPELLS AND ARROWS... BUT THERE'S NOT A SINGLE SCRATCH.

DID IT REALLY DIE JUST FROM WILLIAM'S ATTACK?!

IS IT A SEA SNAKE?

WHOA, IT'S HUGE!

IT ATE THE KING!

AISHA! WHERE ARE YOU GOING?!

TO THE BATTLEFIELD!

WE'LL BE MORE USEFUL THERE!

GET OUT OF THE WAY, PLEASE!

LET ME THROUGH!

DON'T WORRY, WILL. I'M SURE I'VE GOT SOME POTION...

TO MAKE IT PUKE OR SOMETHING...?

MONICA GET AWAY FROM THERE!

IT'S DANGEROUS!

LET ME GO, DORIAN!

I NEED TO HELP WILL!

287

AH... WAIT, NO...

THAT'S NOT SAFE EITH--

I'LL HELP YOU!

MONICA, THE SMOKE...!

EVERYBODY GET OUT OF THE WAY,

THINGS MIGHT GET DANGEROUS.

--DAMIEN, WAIT!

AH?!

WHY DID HE DO THAT?

WHY DID WILL SACRIFICE HIMSELF WITH NO HESITATION...?

IS HE DOING THAT BADLY?

AM I THAT BLIND?

WELL, IT DOESN'T MATTER RIGHT NOW...

I'M COMING TO SAVE YOU, WILL.

DAMIEN!

LOOK...

WHAT THE...?

WATCH OUT, DAMIEN.

YOU ALMOST STUCK THE SWORD IN MY FOREHEAD.

WHOAAAA!

HOW?!

WHERE DID YOU COME FROM?!

WILL! YOU'RE FINE!

HE HE, YEAH, TURNS OUT THE MONSTER IS NOT A REAL ONE.

...

I WAS LUCKY ENOUGH TO FALL INTO THE WATER.

THAT WAS SCARY...!

I WAS IN A SEA MADE OF TENTACLES COVERING MY EYES,

ALTHOUGH I WASN'T ABLE TO TOUCH THEM.

I'M GLAD HE'S FINE...

BUT THIS IS REALLY CONFUSING.

DAMIEN!

ARE YOU CRYING?!

UH...

UGH...

COME HERE, GIVE ME A HUG!

I'LL COMFORT YOU!

NO WAY!

IT'S YOUR FAULT. YOU'RE SUCH AN IDIOT!

LOOK, IT'S TRUE!

THE MONSTER IS JUST A MIRAGE!

I CAN WALK THROUGH IT LIKE IT'S NOTHING!

BUT... WHO WOULD DO SUCH A THING?

AND...WHY?

THAT'S WHY IT HASN'T DESTROYED THE HOUSE OR ANYTHING ELSE!

...

...

DORIAN!

AH...!

DANI...!

THEY'VE USED THE MONSTER AS A DISTRACTION!

WITCHES, CLEARLY.

AND WE STUPIDLY FELL FOR IT.

WE MUST FIND HER, BEFORE THEY TAKE HER TOO FAR AWAY!

I WON'T LOSE DANI AGAIN!

I THINK SOMEONE TOOK HER!

AH!

THEY'RE TAKING HER AWAY!

PERHAPS THEY'RE TAKING HER TO SAVE HER FROM THE MONSTER.

HEY, MARK, OVER HERE!

BARRY!

WHERE'D YOU COME FROM?

DANI!

THESE WITCHES ARE WELL-KNOWN FOLLOWERS OF ANGELA AND HANS...

THEY ATTEMPTED TO CANCEL OUR NEWSPAPER MULTIPLE TIMES.

WE TRIED TO STOP THEM, AND IF IT WASN'T FOR NOAH,

I'M PRETTY SURE THE WITCHES WOULD BE MILES AWAY BY NOW.

ARE YOU OKAY?

YEAH... I'M FINE...

WE DON'T WANNA HURT YOU!

JUST LEAVE US ALONE.

LET US GO AND IT'LL ALL BE FINE.

ARGH!

SARAH! ARE YOU ALL RIGHT?!

OH, COME ON!

WHO...?

IT'S FUNNY.

'CAUSE IF YOU WON'T GIVE MY SISTER BACK...

I DO INTEND TO HURT YOU QUITE A BIT.

LISTEN, BOB, THAT GUY... THAT GUY'S A WYTTE.

THE OLDER BROTHER IS ALSO THERE... AND THEY'VE GOT LOTS OF ARMED PEOPLE TOO.

KAT.

STOP IT.

WE WON'T LET YOU KIDNAP HER!

KIDNAP HER?

SHE'S MY SISTER!

SHE'S OUR QUEEN!

AISHA, WILLIAM, FOLLOW ME!

RIGHT NOW?!

THEY'VE ALREADY FALLEN OFF THEIR BROOMS, I CAN FINALLY HERD THEM AS WELL!

YES, RIGHT NOW!

...

AH!

DANI!

NICO, FOLLOW THEM!

GET RID OF THOSE TWO AND HIDE DANI IN A SAFE PLACE.

I'LL TAKE CARE OF THE REST.

SURE!

COME ON, NICO.

UGH...

I NEED TO SCARE THESE FOLKS AWAY.

WHY DID YOU HAVE TO SHOW UP RIGHT NOW?

300

WAAAH, MUM, I DON'T LIKE THE NOISE!

HONEY, DON'T CRY.

THERE'S SO MUCH NOISE OUTSIIIDE!

DON'T BE AFRAID.

THE WITCHES WILL PROTECT US.

AH... MARK, I'M ALSO AFRAID!

AISHA, WHAT ARE YOU LOOKING FOR?

ARROWS!

MONICA TOLD ME TO LOOK FOR ARROWS AND COVER THE TIPS WITH CLOTH.

AH!

THINGS ARE GETTING SERIOUS OUT THERE!

I'M GONNA GO OUT TO SEE IF I CAN HELP.

AHA!

HERE THEY ARE!

HE HE...

THEY ALL HAVE THEIR FEET ON THE GROUND.

301

NOW YOU'LL FIND OUT. YOU'LL SEE WHEN KING WILLIAM ENTERS THE SCENE...

THERE'S NO WAY.

YOU WON'T HURT ANYONE WITH THAT SWORD.

WHAT'S WITH THE HAT?

I'M NOT A WITCH LIKE YOU, MONICA...

THAT WE CAN BE GOOD MONARCHS.

WE WILL.

IT'S A SYMBOL.

IT MEANS THAT WE'RE NOT DIFFERENT FROM THEM.

NOT ANYMORE.

WE'LL FIGHT TO GET DANI BACK, BUT ALSO TO ACHIEVE PEACE.

IT MEANS THAT WE'RE NOT OUR FATHERS.

A...

A FROG?

IT'S A DRAGON FROG!

RUUUUN!

CRUSH THEM, CARLO!

PHEW...

AND YOU, DANI...

I WAS HOPING THE BROOM RACE HAD ACCOMPLISHED SOMETHING, BUT IT HASN'T...

WE NEED TO TAKE YOU TO A SAFE PLACE, DANI.

LET'S GO!

ARE YOU OK?

LOOK, THE QUEEN IS RIGHT THERE!

I THINK MY LEG'S HURT...

306

308

313

OF COURSE.

WHAT...?

IT WASN'T ME...

THERE WAS SOMEONE ELSE THERE.

I'M SURE YOU DIDN'T EVEN KNOW WHAT YOU WERE DOING.

IT HAS ALWAYS BEEN YOUR SPECIALTY, DOING STUFF WITHOUT MEANING TO.

ALL THIS TIME...

IT WAS YOU ALL ALONG.

YOU...

YOU'VE CURSED YOURSELF, HAVEN'T YOU?

OH, DANI...

MY DANI...

HOW CLUMSY.

315

HURRY UP, WE NEED TO GET NICO OUT OF THERE!

YES...

ALTHOUGH IT'D BE GOOD FOR DANI TO STAY INSIDE AS WE SCARE THESE PEOPLE AWAY.

I CAN'T THINK OF A SAFER PLACE.

ALL RIGHT, I'M GONNA OPEN A HOLE IN THE STONE.

DON'T LET ANY WITCH GO NEAR THE STONE FORTRESS!

DISENCHANT THE QUEEN.

UNDO YOUR SPELL.

NOW.

WAIT, DORIAN!

DON'T ATTACK HIM!

DORIAN, NO...!

NOT LIKE THIS!

I WON'T ASK TWICE.

ALL RIGHT!

ALL RIGHT, I'M LETTING HER GO!

AH...!

NO!

LEAVE HIM ALONE!

WHY ARE YOU SO CRUEL?

WE ONLY WANTED OUR QUEEN!

WE DON'T WANT TO GO BACK TO HOW IT WAS BEFORE...

BECAUSE OF HER...

WE COULD WALK THE STREETS WITHOUT ANY FEAR FOR THE FIRST TIME.

THANKS TO HER, WE STOPPED HIDING WHO WE ARE.

DANI...

YOU'RE SO SELFISH.

DANI, I...

I'VE FORGOTTEN SOMETHING IMPORTANT, HAVEN'T I?

WHAT IF WE COULD CHANGE IT?

WHAT IF WE COULD FIX IT ALL WITH OUR WILLPOWER?

WHAT WOULD YOU THINK OF ME NOW?

'CAUSE YOU NEVER DID ANYTHING WRONG.

NEVER.

I FEEL LIKE I'VE DISAPPOINTED YOU.

FOR JUST A SECOND, I'D LIKE TO STOP FEELING ANYTHING, ONCE AND FOR ALL.

ONCE AGAIN.

I THINK NICO...

...IS DYING.

WHA...?

BA-DUMP

BA-DUMP

NICO!

NO...

BA-DUMP

EVERYTHING SPILLED...

NICO, LOOK AT ME! ARE YOU AWAKE?!

MMMH...

BA-DUMP

LET ME SEE...

AH!

HE'S LOSING A LOT OF BLOOD!

WHAT SHOULD WE DO...?

BA-DUMP

I'M FINE, I'M FINE.

DORIAN, LISTEN...

CAN YOU HEAL HIM WITH MAGIC, DORIAN?

NO...

I DON'T KNOW...

BA-DUMP

DANI WOULD BE BACK...

WITHOUT HER POWERS, THOUGH.

PERHAPS THIS IS WHAT SHE WANTS. SHE WAS NEVER ENTIRELY HAPPY WITH THEM EITHER.

ALTHOUGH...

WHY DOES IT HURT SO MUCH TO THINK OF IT?

WHAT ELSE CAN WE DO?

DANI...

... ALL RIGHT.

COUGH

COUGH

COUGH

NICO!

WE NEED TO FIND SOMEONE WHO'S ABLE TO HEAL HIM.

THERE ARE MANY WITCHES, MAYBE SOMEONE CAN HELP.

NICO? ARE YOU THERE? SPEAK TO ME, SAY SOMETHING...

TELL MARK I CAN SMELL HIS ARMPITS...

THE VILLAGE IS A WRECK...

329

THEY HAVEN'T STOPPED FIGHTING... WITCHES AGAINST WITCHES.

THIS DOESN'T MAKE ANY SENSE.

WHAT ARE WE GONNA DO?

I DON'T KNOW...

THAT'S ENOUGH!

EVERYBODY.

STOP.

CAN'T YOU SEE WHAT YOU'RE DOING?!

YOU FIGHT FOR THE FREEDOM OF WITCHES...

BY ATTACKING OTHER WITCHES?!

IT'S OVER.

IT'S NOT OVER.

WE WANT OUR QUEEN.

330

LET'S MAKE A DEAL.

WE HEAL YOUR FRIEND.

YOU GIVE US OUR QUEEN AND ALLOW US TO LEAVE.

WE WON'T BOTHER YOU ANYMORE. WE'LL LEAVE AND LIVE OUR LIFE FAR AWAY.

WHERE NOBODY WILL LOCK US UP OR BURN US.

WE NEED THE QUEEN, THOUGH.

SHE'S OUR SYMBOL, THE LIGHT OF A TORCH THAT'LL GUIDE WHOEVER IS LOOKING FOR A BETTER PLACE.

WE WON'T ALLOW YOU TO LOCK HER UP.

DANIELA WYTTE IS MY SISTER. WE JUST WANT TO HEAL HER.

WE NEED TO
BE BETTER THAN
THAT.

STOP
BLABBERING!

DO YOU THINK I
WEAR THIS 'CAUSE
IT'S COOL?!

WELL, MAYBE
JUST A LITTLE.
IT LOOKS REALLY
CUTE ON ME.

BUT IT'S ALSO MY SYMBOLIC GESTURE TOWARDS YOU.

TOWARDS EVERYONE!

WE AREN'T GONNA LOCK ANYBODY UP!

NOT THOSE WHO DO MAGIC AND NOT YOUR QUEEN.

YOU CAN REST ASSURED.

SORRY IF I CAN'T ACTUALLY TRUST YOU...

YOUR FRIEND IS WOUNDED.

MINE TOO.

WE'RE ALL IN THE SAME BOAT.

THIS CLEARLY GOT A BIT OUT OF HAND.

PROMISE ME NOBODY IN MY GROUP WILL END UP IN THE DUNGEONS.

WELL...

ALMOST NOBODY.

OF COURSE.

I SWEAR.

UH...

THANK YOU SO MUCH.

AND HOW MANY HAVE BECOME INTERESTED IN MAGIC OVER THE LAST COUPLE OF YEARS?

AND WHAT DOES IT MATTER, WHO STARTED FIRST AND WHO CAME LATER?

WE WERE ALL...

IDIOTS.

WE WERE ALL IDIOTS.

WE CAN CREATE SOMETHING NEW, THOUGH, ALL TOGETHER.

SOMETHING STRONGER AND BETTER.

WE'LL START BY RECONSTRUCTING THE VILLAGE,

JUST LIKE WE DID WITH THE MASTER'S HOUSE.

OH, THAT'S A GOOD IDEA!

MY HOUSE WAS TOTALLY SHATTERED!

WILL IT BE FREE?

THE FAÇADE OF MY HOUSE COULD REALLY USE A COAT OF PAINT.

IF YOU WANDER OFF, THE CYCLE WILL START AGAIN.

YOU DON'T NEED TO FEAR THE FUTURE.

I WAS ALSO SCARED.

BUT FEAR ISN'T FOREVER.

STAY HERE. SHARE.

MIX. COEXIST.

AND THEN PAST FEAR WON'T COME BACK.

NOT IF WE ALL STICK TOGETHER.

IT DOESN'T HAVE TO BE ALL BLACK AND GLOOMY.

HA-HA!

OH?

MY LATE FATHER-IN-LAW FORBADE PUNISHING WITCHES FOR DOING MAGIC.

IT WAS MANY YEARS AGO,

ALTHOUGH SOME PEOPLE LIKE MY FATHER DIDN'T RESPECT THAT RULE.

MONICA AND I, AS THE NEW QUEEN AND KING, ARE GOING TO TAKE A STEP FORWARD.

STARTING FROM NOW,

MAGIC WILL BE FOR EVERYONE.

I DID ALL I COULD...

NOW HE NEEDS TO REST...

THANK YOU SO MUCH, REALLY.

AH...

OH... HOW LOVELY...

DORIAN...?

MMM?

IS IT REALLY YOU?

OF COURSE IT'S ME.

DANI?

BUT... I THINK I SAW YOU DIE...

YOU GOT BURNED.

I...

WAS IT A DREAM?

DID I MAKE IT ALL UP?

NO, YOU DIDN'T MAKE IT UP.

IT HAPPENED, BUT THAT WASN'T ME.

THIS IS REAL.

DANIII!

AH!

WE'VE MISSED YOU!

I'M SO GLAD YOU'RE BACK!

AW, I LOVE YOUR SMILE! YOU LOOK SO DIFFERENT NOW!

DAMIEN.

GO GIVE OUR SISTER A HUG.

COME ON.

NO.

HUUUH?

WHY NOT?!

COME ON, DON'T BE SHY!

I SAID NO! SHE'LL THINK I'M WEIRD!

I'M GLAD YOU'RE OK!

THANK YOU, ANNE!

WAS I NOT DOING WELL?

ARGH!

DANI!

ARE YOU OK?

YES, I JUST TRIPPED OVER...

...MY HAIR?

WHAT...?

THIS HAIR IS STUPIDLY LONG.

AH! AND WHAT ABOUT THIS DRESS?!

I LOOK OLD!

NOW THAT YOU'RE NOT AN EVIL OVERLADY ANYMORE, IT DOESN'T SUIT YOU, TO BE HONEST.

SO YOU HAVE NO MEMORY AT ALL OF THE LAST THREE YEARS?

AH, HI DAMIEN.

I THINK...

...I DO?

I'M NOT SURE. I FEEL DIZZY...

AH...

WAIT.

NICO!

WELL, HE'S STILL UNCONSCIOUS.

HE HAS STOPPED BLEEDING THOUGH.

AH...

MAJESTY.

WAIT.

DANI JUST WENT THROUGH A MAJOR SHOCK.

SHE NEEDS TO REST.

WE ALL DO.

LET'S TAKE SOME TIME TO REGAIN OUR STRENGTH.

WE WILL MEET LATER.

MY HUSBAND AND I HAVE AN OFFER FOR YOU.

THOSE WITCHES RECONSTRUCTED THE ROOFTOP IN JUST A FEW MINUTES.

AMAZING!

WITH THEIR HELP WE WILL FINISH IN NO TIME!

WE NEED MORE STONE. THESE FACADES ARE TOTALLY WRECKED.

WILL THERE BE ENOUGH MONEY?

KING WILLIAM SAID HE'LL TAKE CARE OF THE EXPENSES.

IT TURNS OUT HE'S A GOOD GUY AFTER ALL.

HE HAS SOME GUTS, THAT'S FOR SURE!

349

TODAY YOU WERE THE MOST AMAZING PERSON I'VE EVER SEEN.

AND, WELL, I... UH...

THAT'S IT.

WE SHOULD GO TO THE MEETING WITH MONICA AND THE WITCHES.

WAIT, DAMIEN!

I...

YOU...

MAYBE YOU WERE RIGHT.

I MIGHT BE ABLE TO WEAR THE CROWN PROUDLY AND DO A GOOD JOB.

MAYBE IT'S TRUE THAT I CAN BE WORTHY ENOUGH.

AND MOST IMPORTANTLY,

353

NICO!

YOU FINALLY WOKE UP!

GUUUYS, NICO IS AWAKE!

POW

I'M SORRY FOR NOT ANSWERING UNTIL NOW.

I WANTED TO THANK YOU FOR BEING BY MY SIDE, NICO.

FOR NOT LEAVING ME ALONE EVEN THOUGH...

MAYBE I DESERVED IT.

YOU WEREN'T DOING WELL.

I WASN'T GOING TO ABANDON YOU BECAUSE OF THAT.

YOU REMEMBER EVERYTHING, THEN?

WELL...

IT'S WEIRD, A BIT LIKE A DREAM.

GLIMPSES OF FOGGY MEMORIES ARE COMING TO ME, MORE AND MORE.

...

WHAT?

I'M SORRY.

I'M JUST REALLY NERVOUS. I STILL CAN'T BELIEVE IT.

NICO...

HOW WAS THE CURSE BROKEN?

IT HAPPENED WHEN WILLIAM AND MONICA WERE TALKING TO THE PEOPLE.

THEY WERE PROMISING THEM A BETTER FUTURE.

DORIAN MADE A LOT OF COLORFUL HATS FLY,

IT WAS BEAUTIFUL...

AND SUDDENLY I FELT AS IF...

AS IF I HAD BEEN LOCKED INSIDE A SMALL ROOM,

DARK AND DUSTY,

AND THEN A DOOR OPENED, BATHING EVERYTHING WITH LIGHT.

IT WAS LIKE...

...GETTING OUT OF A PRISON CELL.

I FIGURED IT...

IT WASN'T JUST DORIAN'S "DEATH", WAS IT?

WHAT HURT YOU, WHAT MADE YOU WANT TO DISAPPEAR.

IT WAS ALSO ALEX, YOUR DAD,

ALL THE TIMES YOU'VE FELT TRAPPED BETWEEN TWO SIDES IN A TERRIBLE CONFLICT.

YES, YOU'RE RIGHT.

NICO, YOU GOT SO SMART.

I'M NOT SMART.

THIS IS ALL I COULD COME UP WITH IN THREE YEARS.

AND EVEN THEN, IT TOOK ME A WHILE TO REALIZE IT.

NICOOO! YOU'VE SCARED US A LOT!

HEY!

I'M SORRY!

HOW ARE YOU FEELING?

PERFECTLY WELL!

DID YOU SEE?

OUCH!

YES, SHE'S BACK WITH US.

WHAT ON EARTH ARE YOU WEARING, DANI?

AH! I BORROWED IT FROM MARK.

AH! HE BEAT ME TO IT!

MARK, WAIT 'TIL I CATCH YOU...

OF COURSE, MUFFIN BOY.

REGARDLESS, I CAN'T ALLOW YOU TO WEAR THAT.

LUCKILY, YOUR DEAR MONICA IS HERE!

COME, COME, LET'S TRY SOME DRESSES ON.

AH, WAIT...!

NICO, I'M JUST TAKING HER FOR A WHILE.

YOU EXPERIENCED TOO MANY STRONG EMOTIONS IN A SINGLE DAY, AND YOU'RE WOUNDED.

LET YOUR HEART REST FOR A BIT.

...

OHHH, DANI, I'M SO GLAD YOU'RE HERE!

WHOA, SO MANY PEOPLE CAME.

EVEN FROM ANOTHER TOWN, IT SEEMS.

I HOPE IT'LL BE FINE.

I HOPE SO TOO...

DON'T WORRY, GUYS...

THIS TIME AROUND, I'M TAKING A QUEEN WITH ME.

AS SOON AS THEY SEE DANI, THEY'LL LISTEN.

I THINK I'M GONNA FAINT.

CHEER UP, DANI!

YOU LOOK STUNNING.

THANK YOU, GIRLS.

YES, I LIKE IT.

YOU DID A GREAT JOB.

COULD YOU BY ANY CHANCE SEND AN EMISSARY TO MY PALACE?

THANKS!

I DID IT WITH DORIAN AND DAMIEN. WE ALL SHARE THE CREDIT.

I'D LIKE TO IMPLEMENT THIS PROJECT.

THIS IS SO INTERESTING, MONICA...

IN MY KINGDOM, WE HAVEN'T EXPERIENCED ANY DISCRIMINATION BETWEEN WITCHES AND NON-WITCHES IN A LONG TIME, BUT STILL...

SERIOUSLY?

CONSIDER IT DONE!

HEY, DANI. ARE YOU READY?

DORIAN...!

HEY, WE'RE MATCHING!

I KNOW! IT COULDN'T BE ANY OTHER WAY.

WE WILL MAKE AN IMPECCABLE IMPRESSION ON THE PEOPLE.

HOW ARE YOU FEELING? NERVOUS?

I NEED TO CONVINCE ALL THOSE PEOPLE NOT TO KILL MONICA, AND THEREUPON ABDICATE IN HER FAVOR.

INCREDIBLY.

DON'T WORRY.

IF I SEE YOU STRUGGLE, I'LL BE THERE TO CHANGE A FEW HAT COLORS HERE AND THERE!

THANK YOU SO MUCH, DORIAN!

JUST THINK THAT AFTER THIS, YOU WON'T BE THE QUEEN ANYMORE.

YOU WILL BE FREE TO MAKE YOUR OWN DECISIONS.

MY DECISIONS...?

HOW ABOUT YOU, DORIAN?

DANI, HURRY UP,

YOU NEED TO GO OUT AT THE SAME TIME AS MONICA!

HAVE YOU DECIDED WHAT YOU WANT TO DO?

YES, I'VE MADE UP MY MIND.

COME ON, DANI. THEY'RE WAITING FOR YOU.

GET READY AS WELL, DORIAN.

...

THANK YOU ALL SO MUCH FOR COMING HERE TODAY.

WE HAVE A BIG ANNOUNCEMENT TO MAKE.

SOMETHING THAT WILL CHANGE THE WORLD FOREVER.

RUN, JULIA!

WE'RE GONNA MISS THE BUS!

JUST DON'T RUN SO FAST!

OH NO, IT'S LEAVING ALREADY!

I CAN ONLY COME UP WITH ONE THING.

WAAAIT!

HURRY UP, GET ON THE BROOM.

WAIT, KIDS...

THAT'S DANGEROUS...

OH!

WHOA!

AWESOME!

WE COULDN'T MISS THE FIRST DAY OF CLASS!

HEY, YOU! WHAT DO YOU THINK YOU'RE DOING?

THAT WAS DANGEROUS!

THANK YOU FOR STOPPING!

THANKS!

YEAH, BUT YOU DIDN'T NEED TO GO SO FAST ON THAT BROOM...

IT'S NOT LIKE THE SCHOOL IS HIDDEN.

GOOD MORNING, EVERYONE.

AS YOU KNOW, THIS COURSE IS PART OF A GREAT EDUCATIONAL REFORM.

HOW HANDSOME...

I HOPE HE'S GONNA BE OUR NEW TUTOR...

STARTING NOW, A NUMBER OF SUBJECTS WILL BE ADDED,

INCLUDING POTION-MAKING, FLYING ON A BROOM,

ELEMENTAL SPELLS, DOMESTIC SPELLS, DIVINATION, AND SO FORTH...

HOW DID IT GO? DID YOU TALK?

HE ASKED ME...

IF WE'RE READY TO GO AND SEE MUM.

...

... YES.

WE SHOULD GO.

DAMIEN!

GOOD MORNING.

YOU'RE LATE.

SORRY TO KEEP YOU WAITING.

WOW! WHAT'S WITH THE OUTFIT?

DID YOU DRESS UP LIKE THAT FOR MUM?

SHUT UP.

...

WHAT HAPPENED WITH THE PRISONERS OF WAR, DAMIEN?

AS FOR THE OTHERS, WELL...

THOSE WHO DID NOT COMMIT VIOLENT CRIMES WON'T RECEIVE ANY CHARGES.

MOST OF THEM HAVE BEEN DEPORTED AND DEPRIVED OF THEIR MAGICAL POWERS.

AUNT HILDE SAID THAT SHE DIDN'T CARE IF SHE LOST HER MAGIC,

BUT STILL, SINCE SHE WAS ONE OF THE LEADERS, SHE HAD TO PAY A LARGE SUM OF MONEY AS COMPENSATION.

THOSE FUNDS WILL GO DIRECTLY TO THE SCHOOL.

AUNT HILDE...

AND WHERE IS SHE NOW?

POOR THING, SHE REALLY LOVED HER MONEY.

I HEARD THAT SHE SET UP A POTION BUSINESS IN THE OUTSKIRTS OF THE KINGDOM.

IT'S GOING PRETTY WELL.

UM...

WHAT ABOUT THE MASTER? IS HE STILL IN JAIL?

PENDRAGON...

HE WAS BROKE, BUT HE WAS DEPRIVED OF HIS POWERS AND DEPORTED.

HE LEFT SILENTLY, WITH HIS HEAD LOW.

WE HAVEN'T HEARD ABOUT HIM EVER SINCE.

I DON'T THINK...

WE'LL EVER SEE HIM AGAIN.

AND THEN THERE'S HER,

ANGELA WYTTE.

MUM.

HELLO, MUM.

DAMIEN!

GOOD MORNING!

YOU'RE A BIT LATE TODAY!

I KNOW, I'M SORRY.

I HAD SOMETHING TO DO.

HAVE YOU ALREADY HAD BREAKFAST, SWEETHEART?

NO, OF COURSE NOT.

WE'RE GONNA HAVE BREAKFAST TOGETHER AS ALWAYS, RIGHT?

AH...

OH, WELL, I HAVE ALREADY EATEN! I'M SORRY!

OH, COME ON...!

...

HI, MUM.

MUM!

DORIAN...

DANI...

YOU CAME...

I'M GLAD TO SEE YOU'RE FINE.

DANI, SWEETHEART...

WHAT HAPPENED?

I DON'T KNOW.

BUT EVERYTHING'S OKAY NOW.

...

MUM, DANI AND I ARE LIVING TOGETHER CLOSE BY.

I THOUGHT YOU COULD ALSO SETTLE...

DORIAN.

MUM IS GONNA LIVE HERE WITH ME, AT THE PALACE.

SHE'LL BE FINE. THERE'S NOTHING TO WORRY ABOUT.

SHE WON'T BE LOCKED UP.

IT'S NOT A PROBLEM FOR ME AT ALL.

SHE'S MY MOTHER.

AND ALSO MINE.

I'VE ALLOWED YOU TO TAKE ALL THE RESPONSIBILITY FOR WAY TOO LONG.

YOU NEED TO GET ON WITH YOUR LIVES. YOU'RE STILL KIDS.

LET ME DO THIS.

MOREOVER, I LIKE HAVING HER HERE.

COME ON,

GIVE HER A HUG.

SHE SAYS SHE HAS NOWHERE TO GO,

BECAUSE IT DOESN'T MAKE SENSE TO BE SEPARATED FROM HER KIDS.

PERHAPS, LITTLE BY LITTLE, OVER TIME...

WE'LL MANAGE TO BE A FAMILY AGAIN.

I'M OFF TO SCHOOL, DANI.

WHAT ARE YOU UP TO TODAY?

AH? WELL, I SUPPOSE...

NOTHING.

I'LL CRASH ON THE SOFA.

BYE!

COME ON, DON'T SAY THAT.

WHEN I'M BACK, WE COULD GO FOR A NOCTURNAL PICNIC.

...

SOUNDS GOOD...

BUT...

BUT I CAN'T GO ON LIKE THIS.

DORIAN, MONICA, DAMIEN, WILLIAM, MARK, EVEN NICO...

EVERYONE ELSE IS MAKING DECISIONS, LIVING THEIR LIVES, AND DOING GREAT AND KIND THINGS.

WHAT CAN I DO, THOUGH?

I NEED TO STOP BEING LAZY AND MAKE UP MY MIND!

I GOT IT! ONLY ONE PLACE CAN HELP ME FIGURE OUT MY FUTURE!

THAT'S ALL FOR TODAY!

SEE YOU TOMORROW, PROFESSOR WYTTE!

HI, PROFESSOR WYTTE!

ARE YOU FREE TO GO ON A DATE WITH ME YET?

MONICA!

WHAT ARE YOU DOING HERE?!

IF THE CHILDREN DISCOVER US, IT WILL BE A DISASTER!

SO YOU'RE ENJOYING YOUR LIFE AS A TEACHER?

I LOVE IT!

SEEING THE CHILDREN'S PROGRESS IN MAGIC IS WONDERFUL.

AND I SPEND MOST OF MY TIME READING!

I'M BUILDING MY DREAM LIBRARY AT HOME!

I'LL BORROW YOUR FAVORITE NOVELS, THEN!

I DON'T HAVE ANY...

I THINK NOVELS ARE A WASTE OF TIME. YOU CAN'T LEARN ANYTHING FROM THEM.

ARE YOU KIDDING?!

THEY'VE INSPIRED ME AND MADE ME GROW!

READ SOME OF THEM, YOU WON'T REGRET IT!

I'LL READ THEM ALL.

IN NOVELS YOU CAN LEARN ABOUT LIFE, ABOUT THE VERY ESSENCE OF HUMAN BEINGS!

WHAT?!

I LOVE HOW PASSIONATE YOU ARE ABOUT IT.

I WANT US TO EXPERIENCE TOGETHER THE THINGS THAT MAKE YOU HAPPY!

DORIAN...

AH!

I'M EXPERIENCING A SECRET, FORBIDDEN LOVE STORY.

HOW EXCITING!

DO YOU THINK I'M THE WORST FOR ENJOYING THIS SO MUCH?

I THINK YOU READ TOO MANY NOVELS.

HA-HA!

377

I ROUGHLY KNOW THE MEANING, BUT THEY'RE NOTHING MORE THAN ARCHETYPES AND...

ARE YOU PAYING ATTENTION?

WHAT DOES THE FOOL MEAN?!

UM...

IT STANDS FOR SOMETHING LIKE...

A FREE SPIRIT, INNOCENCE, THE START OF SOMETHING NEW...

IT COULD POSSIBLY INDICATE A TRIP OR...?

NICO, YOU'VE ENLIGHTENED ME!

WHAT? THIS FAST?

THIS CARD REPRESENTS A JOURNEY...

AND LOOK, THERE'S A SUN IN THE PICTURE!

THE LIGHT OF A TORCH THAT'LL GUIDE WHOEVER IS LOOKING FOR A BETTER PLACE.

THAT'S ME!

DANI, YOU'RE THE IDEAL CLIENT OF ANY SCAM TAROT-READER.

NO, LISTEN!

THAT'S MY MISSION, TO FINISH WHAT I STARTED WHEN I WAS UNDER THE SPELL!

I HAVE TO VISIT OTHER KINGDOMS AND BRING THEM MONICA'S VISION FOR A SCHOOL OF FREE MAGIC FOR EVERYONE.

TO PREVENT BAD THINGS FROM HAPPENING AGAIN IN THE FUTURE.

YOU MEAN YOU WANT TO...

LEAVE?

NO, NO...

WELL, JUST A LITTLE.

BUT I'M PRETTY FAST WITH THE BROOM.

PERHAPS I'LL BE GONE FOR A FEW WEEKS FROM TIME TO TIME.

EH, NICO...

NO, IT'S OKAY...

IT'S JUST THAT IT MAKES ME SAD.

YOU'VE BEEN COMING HERE EVERY DAY LATELY.

I JUST CAN'T REMAIN UNEMPLOYED FOREVER.

...

RIGHT...

UH...

LISTEN, DANI... I...

THERE'S SOMETHING...

I MUST TELL YOU.

380

381

DO YOU ALREADY KNOW EVERYTHING BY HEART, DANI?

YES!

WELL, MORE OR LESS.

I'LL STUDY ON THE WAY. I PROMISE!

JUST IN CASE YOU FORGET SOMETHING, YOU'VE GOT MY SIGNED REPORTS.

ALTHOUGH, ANYONE WOULD WANT TO STUDY MAGIC JUST BY LOOKING AT THAT ADORABLE OUTFIT.

YOU'RE THE BEST MESSENGER I COULD WISH FOR!

AND YOU DIDN'T ORDER A UNIFORM FOR NICO, MONICA?

I WANTED TO SEE IT.

I WON'T BE WORKING AS A MESSENGER!

I'M ONLY GOING WITH DANI TO EARN SOME CASH FROM UNWISE NEW CLIENTS.

YEAH, I'M SURE THAT'S THE MAIN REASON WHY YOU'RE GOING WITH HER...

AH! HELLO WILLIAM. HI DAMIEN!

SEE? SHE HASN'T LEFT YET!

I TOLD YOU!

DAMIEN WAS AFRAID YOU LEFT BEFORE HE COULD SAY GOODBYE, DANI.

HUH?

REALLY?

DON'T WORRY, I'M ONLY GONNA BE GONE FOR A FEW WEEKS!

YEAH, BUT IT'S YOUR FIRST TRIP ON YOUR OWN AS A MESSENGER...

I THOUGHT I COULD GIVE YOU SOME ADVICE, PERHAPS... AS YOUR OLDER BROTHER...

I'M NOT GOING ON MY OWN!

NICO IS COMING WITH ME.

HEY!

...

THEN I'M GONNA GIVE A PIECE OF ADVICE TO YOU INSTEAD...

HEY, YOU'RE FREAKING ME OUT!

YES,
I'M SURE
OF IT.

I WILL
KEEP ON DOING
MY BEST.

WE ALL
WILL.

WE WILL WORK
TOGETHER

WITH WHAT WE
HAVE, WITH EVERYTHING
WE HAVE LEARNED.

SO THAT, LITTLE
BY LITTLE,

WE WILL BE
ABLE TO RECTIFY
PAST MISTAKES,

AND CREATE A
BETTER WORLD FOR
EVERYONE.

THE END

•EPILOGUE•

TELL ME, MY DEAR CHILDREN...

HOW ARE YOUR LOVE LIVES GOING?

COME ON, DON'T BE SHY!

TELL YOUR MOM ABOUT YOUR BOYFRIENDS AND GIRLFRIENDS!

I'M SINGLE.

OF COURSE, YOU'RE STILL VERY YOUNG, DANI.

AND SO IS DORIAN.

BUT MY DAMIEN HAS ALREADY REACHED MARRIAGEABLE AGE.

TELL ME, SWEETHEART, IS THERE A GIRL WHO HAS STOLEN YOUR HEART?

HOW AM I SUPPOSED TO TELL HER?

NO, THERE'S NO GIRL...

PERFECT, BECAUSE I'VE BEEN THINKING...

SINCE WE'RE NOW FOLLOWING THIS "PEACEFUL" ROUTE AND YOU THREE HAVE CONNECTIONS TO ROYALTY...

YOU, DAMIEN, COULD SEDUCE MONICA.

THEN DANI COULD SEDUCE KING WILLIAM...

...AND WE, THE WYTTES, WILL GET ALL THE POWER OF THE CROWN.

IT'S AN EXCELLENT PLAN...

OH, IT'S FUNNY YOU SHOULD MENTION THAT, MOM...

ACTUALLY, WE HAVE A SLIGHTLY DIFFERENT SUGGESTION.

FARMERS KEEP COMPLAINING THAT SOME FIELDS ARE STILL BARREN BECAUSE OF THE MAGIC WARS.

AHA...

I SUGGEST THAT MONICA SET UP RESEARCH IN HER POTIONS LAB TO FIND SOMETHING THAT CAN RETURN FERTILITY TO THE LAND.

SOUNDS GOOD.

HOWEVER, THERE IS SOMETHING IMPORTANT I WOULD LIKE TO CONSULT YOU ON, DAMIEN...

WHAT?

I WOULD LIKE TO REWARD YOUR LOYALTY AS A ROYAL ADVISER BY TAKING YOU TO DINNER.

WHAT DO YOU SAY?

WILL!

I MEAN...YOUR MAJESTY!

OF COURSE I ACCEPT YOUR HONORABLE REWARD.

DO THOSE TWO EVEN TRY TO HIDE ANYTHING ANYMORE?

POOR QUEEN MONICA, WHAT A HUSBAND...

I HEARD THAT SHE ALSO HAS A WITCH BOY AS A VERY GOOD FRIEND.

393

EPILOGUE 3

AH, THERE YOU ARE!

MONICA TOLD ME YOU WANTED TO SEE ME!

YES... I NEED TO TALK TO YOU...

HA HA HA HA

WHAT ARE YOU DOING WITH YOUR SHIRT ALL BUTTONED UP?

I DON'T KNOW, MONICA SAID IT LOOKS BETTER LIKE THIS.

TO CONQUER A GIRL'S HEART, YOU HAVE TO BE CLASSY AND CHIVALROUS!

BUTTON UP YOUR SHIRT, NICO!

AND GOOD LUCK!

MONICA HAS NO IDEA!

IT DOESN'T SUIT YOU.

AH!

EPILOGUE 4

THE QUEEN GETS ALONG *REALLY* WELL WITH THAT WITCH BOY. RIGHT, YOUR MAJESTY?

HUH?

> WELL, THIS IS IT!
>
> THANK YOU SO MUCH FOR READING THIS FAR. I HOPE YOU ENJOYED READING *HOOKY* AS MUCH AS I ENJOYED WRITING IT.

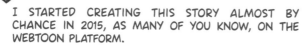

I STARTED CREATING THIS STORY ALMOST BY CHANCE IN 2015, AS MANY OF YOU KNOW, ON THE WEBTOON PLATFORM.

AND IN EARLY 2020 I FINISHED DRAWING THE ADVENTURES OF DANI AND DORIAN. AT THE TIME I'D ALREADY SAID GOODBYE TO THEM (AND TO THE READERS!), AND I DIDN'T THINK THAT THREE YEARS LATER I WOULD BE SAYING GOODBYE TO THEM AGAIN AND PROBABLY FOR GOOD.

THE TRUTH IS THAT I STILL FIND IT HARD TO BELIEVE!

HOOKY HAS BEEN WITH ME FOR EIGHT YEARS OF MY LIFE! IT HAS MEANT A LOT OF WORK AND DEDICATION. FIRST, IN WEBTOON, I WROTE AND DREW ONE EPISODE PER WEEK. THE TRUTH IS THAT THE DEADLINES SOMETIMES WERE A STRUGGLE FOR ME. THEN, I HAD TO TRANSLATE THE WHOLE STORY INTO THE LANGUAGE OF TRADITIONAL COMICS. THIS MEANT DOING A REVISION AND REORGANIZATION OF ABSOLUTELY EVERYTHING.

> BUT IT WAS WORTH EVERY MINUTE OF IT. TO BE ABLE TO SHARE MY STORIES WITH THE WORLD AND SEE THAT ON THE OTHER SIDE, OTHERS ENJOY THEM WITH THE SAME INTENSITY AS I DO, IS SOMETHING ABSOLUTELY WONDERFUL.

THANK YOU SO MUCH FOR YOUR SUPPORT. TRULY.

FOR EVERY COMMENT ON WEBTOON AND ON MY SOCIAL MEDIA, FOR EVERY VIDEO EDIT, FOR EVERY FANART, FOR EVERY TIME YOU CAME TO THE SIGNINGS AND TOLD ME HOW MUCH YOU LIKED THE STORY, OR HOW MUCH YOU LOVED THIS OR THAT CHARACTER. I'M DELIGHTED WHEN YOU TELL ME THAT MY STORY HAS ENCOURAGED YOU TO CREATE YOUR OWN, OR WHEN YOU CONFESS THAT MY COMIC WAS THE ONE THAT MADE YOU FALL IN LOVE WITH READING.

> YOU ALL MAKE IT ALL MAKE SENSE.

> DANI, DORIAN, AND THE WHOLE GANG WILL ALWAYS HAVE A VERY SPECIAL PLACE IN MY HEART. THEY ARE MY KIDS! I'VE GROWN UP WITH THEM, BOTH AS A PERSON AND AS AN ARTIST. BUT NOW IT'S TIME TO SAY GOODBYE. I'M GOING TO MISS THEM A LOT.

> (ALTHOUGH, TO BE HONEST, I DON'T THINK I'LL BE ABLE TO AVOID DRAWING THEM FROM TIME TO TIME!)

THANKS FOR EVERYTHING,

MÍRIAM BONASTRE TUR
2023

399